"I thought you never used this room…"

Alex's soft breath tickled her neck. "I don't," he whispered. "But I'll make an exception for Brody."

He swept the flashlight over the interior of the room, highlighting baby blue walls, a wooden chest, rocking chair, changing table and…a crib.

She turned her head, stilling as her lips brushed the rough stubble of his jaw. Heart pounding, she fought the desire to nuzzle her cheek against his skin and asked, "Why do you have—"

"Nothing was damaged in here," he said, voice husky. "The crib sheets are in the chest, and once you get Brody settled, you can have my room to yourself for the night."

"But, Alex—"

"Not tonight, okay?" He lowered his head, his mouth moving against her temple and his broad palm settling on her hip. "Let's just get some rest. We all need it."

Of its own accord, her body sank back against his. She fit perfectly, his wide chest and muscular thighs cradling her as though she belonged there.

Had he lost a child?

Was that why he was no longer married?

Dear Reader,

During the toughest times, people usually fall into one of two categories: helpers or hiders.

I've been both.

In 2008, when a tornado hit our little town, I hid in the bathtub. (Which turned out to be a very safe place to be.) But eventually, I had to come out. And the sight of my collapsed roof and crushed car didn't make me feel any better about the situation. Neither did sweeping rainwater out of my kitchen. (I hate housework. Even under the best circumstances.)

But the damage to my property was minor compared to what others suffered. And though lightning and thunder still make me cringe, I don't recall all the moments of panic from that day. What I do remember clearly are the days that followed. The ones when friends and neighbors stopped by to ask if I needed anything. And the ones when I joined a group of friends to help other neighbors restore order to their yards and homes.

Leaving my own wrecked house and problems behind allowed me to help others with theirs. And that changed everything.

In *The Rancher's Miracle Baby*, Tammy Jenkins and Alex Weston are two very different people. One is a helper and one is a hider. At times, those lines blur. But eventually, they both must decide who they really are. And that changes everything.

Thank you for reading.

April

THE RANCHER'S MIRACLE BABY

—

APRIL ARRINGTON

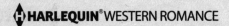
HARLEQUIN® WESTERN ROMANCE

Recycling programs
for this product may
not exist in your area.

ISBN-13: 978-0-373-75772-5

The Rancher's Miracle Baby

Copyright © 2017 by April Standard

Printed in U.S.A.

www.Harlequin.com

April Arrington grew up in a small Southern town and developed a love for movies and books at an early age. Emotionally moving stories have always held a special place in her heart. April enjoys collecting pottery and soaking up the Georgia sun on her front porch.

Visit April at Twitter.com/april_arrington or Facebook.com/authoraprilarrington.

Books by April Arrington

Harlequin Western Romance

Men of Raintree Ranch

Twins for the Bull Rider
The Rancher's Wife
The Bull Rider's Cowgirl

Visit the Author Profile page
at Harlequin.com for more titles.

Dedicated to Patricia B. of Alabama

This writing life is tough. Knowing you're
on the other side of the page changes
everything and helps me make it to The End.
You are a treasured reader, and the world
is a great deal more beautiful with you in it.

Thank you for your sweet messages
and for always reading.

Chapter One

Tammy Jenkins had managed to outrun a lot of things in life. But this had her beat.

"If you're on the road, we urge you to take shelter immediately." The truck's radio crackled, and static scrambled the urgent male voice coming through the speakers. "…summer outbreak…multiple tornadoes spotted. We've received reports of funnel clouds touching down in Leary County, Georgia. The most recent… forming…Deer Creek community."

Deer Creek. Tammy gripped the steering wheel tighter, recalling the crooked green sign she'd passed a few miles back. The bent edges and bullet hole through the center had obscured some of the letters, but the words were legible enough.

A high-pitched neigh and sharp clang split her ears. She glanced in the side-view mirror and cringed as the trailer attached to the truck rocked to one side, squeaking and groaning.

"It's okay, girl," Tammy called out. "I'll find somewhere to stop soon."

Razz, her barrel-racing horse, had experienced her fair share of close calls. And just like when they were about to take a tumble in the arena, the mare sensed danger approaching.

Tammy looked past the trailer and studied the darkening horizon behind them. The wall of black clouds gathered momentum, increasing in size and staining the sky. It swallowed up the dying light of the late-afternoon sun, and a green hue bled through the inky darkness. Thick grass lining both sides of the isolated road rippled with each powerful surge of wind.

Sour acid crept up the back of Tammy's throat, parching her mouth. She jerked her eyes forward, refocused on the road and slammed her foot harder onto the accelerator. The engine rumbled, and the broken yellow line splitting the paved highway streamed by in a blur.

"No need to panic," she said, nodding absently. "It's July. These storms blow over faster than they appear. I'll just have to outrun it before it gets started."

She grinned. If there was one thing she was good at, it was racing. Heck, she didn't have a gold buckle in the glove compartment and over three hundred grand in her savings account for nothing. And there hadn't been a cloud in the sky this morning when she'd left Alabama and crossed the Georgia state line. Chances were, she and Razz would reach their destination earlier than planned.

Her smile slipped. She just wished she'd stayed on the busy interstate instead of cutting through a backwoods town. Especially one that was eerily similar to her rural hometown without a soul in sight.

But the empty road she'd taken was a shortcut. And loneliness had driven her to do what it had always done—made her act before thinking.

A second round of strong kicks rocked the trailer

again and reverberated against the metal walls. The clouds looked darker than ever in the rearview mirror.

Calm down. She straightened and glanced at the trailer. Razz couldn't hear or understand her, but talking to the horse would at least keep Tammy from freaking out.

"We'll pull over somewhere, ride it out and be at Raintree Ranch before you know it, Razz." Tammy forced a laugh, seeking comfort in the sound of her own voice. A strategy she'd been forced to adopt as a child and still utilized at twenty-five. "Jen will be so glad to see you."

Her strained words fell into the empty cab and put a sinking feeling in her stomach. Lord, she wished Jen was with her now, sitting in the passenger seat and teasing her about speeding. A former barrel racer and Tammy's best friend, Jen Taylor had always made traveling the rodeo circuit feel like home. But a year ago, Jen had gotten engaged, retired from racing and settled on Raintree Ranch in Georgia. And for the first time in eight years, Tammy no longer felt like she belonged on the circuit.

Instead, she felt alone. More alone than she cared to admit.

"Suck it up, girl," Tammy muttered, studying the highway. "There's no bawling on Sunday, and there are too many things to be grateful for. Think about taffeta and veils. Flowers and cakes. Rings and vows."

Jen's wedding was worth a bit of bad weather, and with it only a month away, Tammy was determined to be the best dang maid of honor on earth. After scoring another big win in the arena, she'd left the circuit to help Jen finalize seating arrangements, accompany her to a final wedding gown fitting and plan the most fantastic bachelorette party ever known to woman. All in preparation for the bright future awaiting Jen.

A future that included a husband, a home and, eventually, the many children Jen planned to have. Babies Tammy had been asked to serve as godmother to and hoped to shower with love one day.

Tammy's smile returned, her spirits lifting. Her best friend was getting married. Starting a family. "Babies," she whispered.

Fat raindrops splattered against the dusty windshield in quick succession, then stopped as abruptly as they'd begun. Tammy flipped the wipers on, wincing as the rubber jerked noisily over the glass, smearing brown streaks of dirt in her line of vision. A vicious clap of thunder boomed against the ground beneath them and vibrated her sunglasses on the dashboard.

The angry storm wasn't just gaining on them—it was gnashing at their heels.

"It's not that bad, Razz," she said over the rumbles of thunder. "Just a little wind and rain."

Her eyes flicked over the empty landscape surrounding her. There were weeds, trees and fields but no houses or cars. There were no people. No signs of life. And nothing but static left on the radio.

Tammy swallowed hard, mouth trembling. "We need to pull over."

That was what the guy on the radio had said. That was what all news reporters blared in warning as tornadoes approached. It was safer to stop and get out of the vehicle. But the idea of lying facedown in a ditch with nothing but jeans and a T-shirt separating her from the elements was too terrifying to imagine. And there was no way she could leave Razz in the trailer. She needed to find shelter for the mare. A stable or barn. Anything that would give Razz a stronger chance of survival than just running.

"There's got to be something soon." She peered ahead and willed the truck faster up the hill. "We'll just…"

Her voice faded as several white balls tumbled across the road several feet ahead. Some bounced over the pavement and rolled into the grass. Others flew through the air sideways, never touching the ground. Dozens of them. One after the other.

Baseballs…?

She shook her head at the foolish thought, a panicked laugh escaping her. There were no kids playing outside in this weather. And there were no baseball games nearby—

One struck the windshield, punching a hole through the glass and leaving a jagged web of cracks. Tammy stifled a scream and glanced at the passenger seat. Her chest clenched at the thick ball of ice wedged between the door and the seat.

She gritted her teeth and faced forward, blinking rapidly against the wind stinging her eyes through the gaping hole in the windshield. "Everything's okay, Razz." Her voice pitched higher as she shielded her face with one hand. "I'm gonna get us somewhere safe."

The pounding kicks from inside the trailer intensified as hail hammered the truck and trailer. Razz cried out, the sound primal and fierce, and the trailer took a sharp swing to the left.

Tammy grappled with the steering wheel, fighting the wind and managing to redirect the truck's path.

Mercifully, the hail stopped, and she sped over the crest of the hill and down the other side.

Two dirt driveways appeared ahead, one on either side of the road and framed by a line of trees. There were no houses visible, but both roads had to lead somewhere. And wherever they ended, there had to be a better chance of shelter there than on the barren highway.

"Which one?"

Tammy hesitated, eyeing each entrance and catching sight of a wooden fence lining the dirt road on the right. A fence was promising. It meant a house might follow and, hopefully, people.

"Right." She shouted the word, demanding her stiff fingers loosen their death grip on the wheel long enough to make the turn.

She slammed her foot on the accelerator again, turning her face to the side as a fresh surge of rain flew through the busted windshield, smacking against her cheeks. The truck bounced over the uneven ground, jerking her around in the cab and slinging her bottle of soda from the low cup holder to the floorboard.

Tammy ducked her head, rubbed her wet face against her soggy shirtsleeve, then braved the lash of the rain again to scrutinize the end of the driveway.

There was a house, a truck…*and a stable*.

"Thank God," she whispered, jerking the truck to a stop. "We're going to be okay, Razz."

Tammy laid on the horn, then shoved the door open with her shoulder, forcing it out against the wind. No one emerged from the house, and there was no movement outside.

Please. Oh, please let someone be here.

"Help!" She pounded her fist on the horn twice more before jumping out of the cab.

Her boots slid over the slick mud of the driveway, and she gripped the hard metal of the truck, forcing her way through the violent gusts of wind to the trailer.

Razz jerked her head against the open slats. Her dark eyes widened in panic, stark against the black and white markings surrounding them.

"I'm right here." Tammy strived for a calm tone as the spray of wind and rain whipped her bare neck and arms. "I won't leave you."

She ducked her head and continued, making it to the back end and grabbing the latch on the gate. There were deep dents and dings where the hail had hit, making it difficult to pry the door open.

Razz cried out and thrashed against the walls of the trailer. Each panicked act from the horse sent a wave of dread through her.

"I know." Tammy jerked harder at the handle, the bent metal cutting into the sensitive flesh of her palms. "I'm gonna get you out, I promise."

A strange stillness settled around the truck, and the lashing rain stopped. She froze, her hand tightening around the latch.

Moments later, a distant rumble sounded at her back, the rhythmic roar growing louder with each lurch of her heart. Tammy slowly turned and peeled the wet strands of her hair from her eyes with shaky fingers.

There it was. A towering funnel, churning less than a mile away across the landscape, lifting above the hill she and Razz had just traveled over and bearing down on the other side of the road. Its snakelike outline widened with each passing second, growing in size and tearing across the landscape opposite her.

She stood, transfixed, as her eyes tracked its powerful spin. Trees hid its base, but large chunks of debris lifted higher into the air with each second, floating on the outskirts of the black spiral before hurtling to the ground.

The jagged objects were too big and solid to be bits of vegetation. They flipped and twirled like confetti and loose pieces of paper, but they looked firm and heavy. Definitely man-made.

"Oh, no." Tammy's strangled whisper sounded foreign even to her own ears.

Broken beams of wood. Fragmented sections of brick walls. All pieces of a home. There'd been a house at the end of the other driveway, too. And, possibly...*people.*

Her heart stalled. *"No..."*

The trees standing at the base of the twister bent, touched the ground, then disappeared into the black swirl of wind. A fierce chorus of cracks and growls erupted into the air, and the furious churning of wind howled across the field.

Tammy squinted in confusion when the sidetracking motion of the tornado stopped. It was odd. There *was* movement. Large chunks of debris still twirled with the powerful twister, lifting and lowering with each roar of wind. But, somehow, it was standing still.

How could—

Her muscles seized. It wasn't standing still. The twister had shifted its path and was heading across the field again. In her direction.

She spun back to the trailer and jerked on the latch violently. "Help! Please!"

The wind swept away her cry, her lungs burning as Razz's kicks rocked the trailer.

Tammy squatted low and yanked harder on the handle, her heart hammering painfully. She needed to run to the house. But to leave Razz without a chance—

"Please." She pulled harder, her arms screaming in protest.

A shrill noise erupted at her side. Something flashed in the air—flat and silver—then slammed into her temple, knocking her to the ground.

Tammy blinked hard, a sharp pain slicing through her head and a flash of light distorting her vision. Wetness trickled down her cheek.

Touching a trembling hand to it, she stared at the dark sky above her and noted the absence of rain. The white spots dancing in front of her eyes cleared, and she pulled her hand from her face and held it up. Red coated her palm.

"It's just blood, Razz," she whispered amid the mare's cries, studying the black clouds through the gaps in her spread fingers.

A hard blow to the head. That was all. Something her father had doled out on a daily basis by the time she'd reached sixteen.

A large shape shifted, moving above her and obscuring the dark clouds. Tammy lowered her palm and her gaze locked with a pair of stormy gray eyes.

A man stared down at her, his broad shoulders and muscled girth blocking the wind. He had tanned skin and black hair sprinkled with silver. The striking mix as deep and rich as the storm overhead.

His big hands reached for her.

"My horse needs help," she rasped, scrambling back.

His piercing gaze cut to the trailer as Razz's kicks and desperate cries strengthened. He swung around, gripped the bent latch and wrestled the gate open. A moment later, Razz burst out of the trailer with disoriented jerks.

"Get," he shouted, smacking the horse's rear.

Razz leaped and took off, galloping out of sight.

"Come on." He yanked Tammy to her feet, tucked her tight to his side and ran across the front lawn toward the house.

Tammy pumped her legs hard, keeping up with his powerful stride and ignoring the nausea roiling in her gut.

The massive surge of wind grew stronger at their backs, and their boots slipped repeatedly on the slick grass. They stumbled up the front steps to the door and fell to the porch floor as the vicious growl of the tornado drew closer.

This is it.

Tammy squeezed her eyes shut, the concrete pressing hard against her cheek and disjointed thoughts whipping through her mind.

She wouldn't make it to Jen's wedding. Wouldn't hug or kiss Jen's children one day. And would never get the chance to have babies of her own. It would remain the foolish dream it'd always been. The kind that belonged to a woman who'd never been able to trust a man with her body or her heart. Unrealistic and unattainable.

"Keep moving." The man's brawny arm tightened around her back as he forced his way to his knees.

Tammy looked up, her eyes freezing on his face. The strong jaw, aquiline nose and sculpted mouth belonged to a stranger. But at least she wasn't alone.

The thought was oddly comforting, and when she spoke, her voice remained steady despite the horrifying possibility she acknowledged.

"We're not going to make it."

THE HELL THEY WEREN'T.

Alex Weston balled his hand into a fist, pressed it to the porch floor and shoved to his haunches. He steadied himself against the strong surge of wind, then reached down and pulled the woman up with him.

She was soft—*and strong.* The slight curves of her biceps were firm underneath the pads of his fingers, and she'd matched his pace as they'd sprinted to the house. But she was slender and light. So light, each gust of wind threatened to steal her from his grasp.

"Keep moving," he growled, ignoring the panicked flare of her green eyes and forging ahead.

Alex shoved her forward and pressed her against the wall of the house. He jerked the front door open and helped her inside, but before he could follow, the wind caught it, ripping it wide-open to the side and yanking him around with it. The sharp edges of brick cut into his back.

Wet grass and dirt sprayed his face, and he spat against it, struggling to maintain control of the door and his panic. He squinted against the bite of wind and peered across the front lawn. The tornado barreled across the driveway toward the house, sucking up the wooden posts of the fence and spitting them out. The wood sliced through the air with shrill whistles, scattering in all directions and stabbing into the ground. Each jagged plank a deadly missile.

His eyes shot to the open field, which was bare and

vulnerable in the path of the twister. He'd just released the horses from their stalls when the woman had driven up. The stable walls were sturdy but no match for the violent storm the weather forecasters had warned against. He'd hoped the horses would have a better chance of surviving if they were free to run. But he had no idea if it'd been the right decision. Was no longer even sure if he would survive the massive twister.

"Hurry."

It was a breathless sound, almost stolen by the wind. The door jerked in his grasp as the woman leaned farther outside, pulling hard on the edge of it.

A high-pitched screech filled the air, and a piece of metal slammed into one of the columns lining the front porch. Adrenaline spiked in his veins, pounding through his blood and burning his muscles. He renewed his grip on the door, and they yanked together, succeeding in wrenching the door closed as they staggered inside.

"This way." Alex grabbed her elbow and darted through the living room, pulling her past the kitchen and down a narrow hallway in the center of the house.

A wry scoff escaped him. His first guest in nine years—other than the Kents living across the road—and he was manhandling her to the floor.

She dropped to her knees, and Alex covered her, tucking her bent form tight to his middle and cupping his hands over the top of her head. They pressed closer to the wall as the violent sounds increased in intensity, filling the dark stillness enfolding them. It was impossible to see anything. But the sounds…

God help him—*the sounds*.

Glass shattered, objects thudded and the savage roar

of the wind obliterated the silence. The house groaned, and the air hissed and whistled in all directions.

Alex's muscles locked, the skin on the back of his neck and forearms prickling. His blood froze into blocks of ice, and his jaw clenched so tight he thought his teeth would shatter.

The damned thing sounded as though it was ripping the house apart. Would rip *them* apart.

Bursts of panicked laughter moved through his chest. This was not how he'd planned to spend his Sunday evening. He'd expected a long day of work on his ranch, a whiskey and an evening spent alone. That was the way it'd been for nine years, since the day his ex-wife left. The way he wanted it. He preferred solitude and predictability.

But there was nothing as unpredictable as the weather. Except for a woman.

"It'll pass." The woman's strained words reached his ears briefly, then faded beneath the ferocious sounds passing overhead. "It'll pass."

Hell if he knew what it was. For some reason, he got the impression she wasn't even speaking to him. That she was simply voicing her thoughts out loud. But something in her tone and the warm, solid feel of her beneath him, breathing and surviving, made the violent shudders racking his body stop. It melted the blocks of ice in his veins, relieving the chill on his skin.

He curled closer, ducked down amid the thundering clang of debris around them and pressed his cheek to the top of the woman's head. Her damp hair clung to the stubble on his jaw, and the musty smell of rain filled his nostrils. Each of her rapid breaths lifted her back tighter against his chest, and the sticky heat of blood from the wound on her temple clung to the pads of his fingers.

"Yeah," he said, his lips brushing her ear as he did his best to shelter her. "It'll pass."

Gradually, the pounding onslaught of debris against the house ceased. The violent winds eased to a swift rush, and the deafening roar faded into the distance. Light trickled down the hallway, and the air around them stilled. The worst of it couldn't have lasted more than forty seconds. But it had felt like an eternity.

"Is it over?"

Alex blinked hard against the dust lingering in the air and lifted his head, focusing on the weak light emanating from the other room. "Yeah." He cleared his throat and sat upright, untangling his fingers from the long, wet strands of her hair. "I think so."

She slipped from beneath him, slumped back against the wall and released a heavy breath. "Thank you."

Her green eyes, bright and beautiful, traveled slowly over his face. His skin warmed beneath her scrutiny, his attention straying to the way her soaked T-shirt and jeans clung to her lush curves and long legs.

He shifted uncomfortably and redirected his thoughts to her age. She looked young. Very young. If he had to guess, he'd say midtwenties…if that. But he'd never been good at pinning someone's age. Just like no one had ever been good at guessing his.

The dash of premature gray he'd inherited made him look older than his thirty-five years. And, hell, to be honest, he felt as old as he probably looked nowadays.

She smiled slightly. "That's pitiful, isn't it?" She shook her head, her low laugh humorless. "A cheap, two-word phrase in exchange for saving my life."

A thin stream of blood flowed from her temple over her flushed cheek, then settled in the corner of her mouth. The tip of her tongue peeked out to touch it, and she frowned.

"Here." Alex tugged a rag from his back pocket and reached for the wound on her head. "It's—"

Her hand shot out and clamped tight around his wrist, halting his movements. "What're you doing?"

He stilled, then lowered his free hand slowly to the floor. Damn, she was strong. Stronger than he'd initially thought. Even though his wrist was too thick for her fingers to wrap around, she maintained control over it. And the panic in her eyes was more than just residual effects from the tornado.

"You're cut." He nodded toward her wound, softening his tone and waiting beneath her hard stare. "You can use this to stop the bleeding."

Her hold on his wrist eased, and her face flooded with color. "Th-thank you."

She took the rag from him and pressed it to her head, wincing at the initial contact, then drew her knees tightly to her chest. He studied her for a moment and touched his other palm to the floor, noting the way she kept eyeing his hands.

"I'm sorry that rag's not clean," he said. "I get pretty sweaty outside during the day." He remained still. "I'm Alex. Alex Weston."

"Tammy Jenkins." She held the rag up briefly. "And thank you again. For everything."

"You've thanked me enough." Cringing at the gruff sound of his voice, he stood slowly and stepped back, his boots crunching over shards of glass. "We better get outside. I need to check the damage to the house before I can be sure it's safe to be in here."

"The house across the road," she said softly, peering up at him. "Did someone live there?"

"Did someone live..." His heart stalled. Dean Kent, his best friend and business partner, lived there. Along with his wife, Gloria, and their eleven-month-old son. "Why? What'd you see?"

"I think it hit that house, too," she said, dodging his eyes and shoving to her feet. "I can't be sure how bad, but it looked like..."

Her voice faded as his boots pounded across the floor, over the porch and down the front steps. The heavy humidity clogged his nose and mouth, making it difficult to breathe, and the frantic sprint made his lungs ache. He jumped over several small piles of debris, registering wood planks, buckets and tree limbs.

He stopped at a twisted pile of metal and absorbed the damage around him. Trees were down everywhere. Some were split in half, the remaining jagged halves stabbing into the air. His stable was in shambles, but, thankfully, the main house seemed somewhat sturdy.

It appeared as though the twister had only sideswiped his house. But Tammy's tone had suggested Dean's house had been hit head-on.

Alex darted toward his truck, but the massive tree lying over the tailgate would take time to move. Precious time he didn't have.

Tammy, breathless, jogged up behind him. "Alex—"

"Do you have your keys?"

She patted her front pocket absently, her wide eyes focused over his left shoulder. "Yes. But they won't do you any good."

He spun and stifled a curse at the sight of her truck and trailer overturned in the mud. Though the worst of the storm had passed, dark clouds still cloaked the sky, and several large drops of rain hit his cheeks and forehead. Another storm approached.

Alex gripped a thick tree limb and hefted himself over the trunk, scrambling over broken branches and shards of glass. He ran as fast as his legs would allow, his boots pounding into puddles of water and mud splashing up his jeans.

A power line was down and crisscrossed the road in a snakelike pattern. He jerked to a halt and stiffened at the sound of feet sloshing over wet ground behind him.

"Wait." He threw out his arm and glanced over his shoulder.

Tammy skittered to a stop, her boots slipping over the mud. Her chest rose and fell with heavy breaths as she surveyed the downed power line.

Alex stood still, each heavy thump of his heart marking the seconds ticking by. *To hell with it.* Dean and Gloria were on the other side. He stepped carefully over each curve of the tangled line until he reached the opposite side of the road.

To his surprise, Tammy followed, her boots taking the same path as his. He waited for her to reach him safely, then they ran the rest of the way to Dean's house.

"Dear God…" His voice left him, and his frantic steps slowed.

There was no longer a two-story house. Just a foundation filled with fragmented brick walls, massive piles of wood, shredded insulation and broken glass. There were no movements and no voices. Only the distant rumble of thunder and random plop of raindrops striking the wreckage filled the silence.

"Dean?" Alex winced. His shaky voice barely rose above the rasp of the wind. He cleared his throat and tried again. *"Dean!"*

No answer. He took a hesitant step forward, then another until he reached the highest pile of rubble, visually sifting through splintered doors, broken window frames and loose bricks. Dread seeped into his veins and weakened his limbs. He began walking the perimeter, struggling to stay upright and fighting the urge to collapse on the wet ground.

Maybe they weren't home. He nodded and kept moving. They might have driven the twenty miles to town to get groceries and could still be there. He rounded what used to be the back of the house and scanned the heaps.

That was what it was—they weren't home. *Thank God.*

"They weren't here," he called out, turning and starting back toward Tammy. "They—"

He froze. The toe of a purple shoe stuck out beneath a toppled, broken brick wall.

Those dang shoes of yours are gonna blind me one day, Gloria.

Alex began to shake. How many times had he heard Dean tease his wife about her purple shoes? The bright ones she liked to run in every morning after they'd fed and turned out the horses?

It's not my shoes that are blinding you, baby, she would chide Dean. *It's my beauty.*

"Gloria?" Alex hit his knees and touched the laces with trembling fingers. He could still hear her laugh in his head. Joyful and energetic. *"Gloria."*

There was no answer. He gripped the edge of the bricks and heaved, barely registering Tammy dropping to his side and lifting with him. They wrestled with the weight of the brick wall, and he counted off, directing Tammy to shove with him in tandem until they managed to shift it. Huge chunks crumbled away, and the largest section broke off to the side, revealing Dean and Gloria underneath.

Lifeless.

"No." Alex shook his head, tuning out Tammy's soft sobs. "This is the wrong one. This is the wrong damned house." He shot to his feet, choked back the bile rising in his throat, then threw his head back to shout up at the dark sky. *"You got the wrong one, you son of a bitch!"*

The storm should've taken his house. It was an empty shell. A pathetic structure that would never shelter children or a married couple—his infertility had seen to the former and his ex-wife had ensured the latter. He wasn't a father or a husband. Hell, he wasn't even a man in the real sense of the word. And there was no bright future to look forward to in his life.

"It should've been me, you bastard," he yelled, his voice hoarse and his throat raw.

Not Gloria. Not Dean. And not…*Brody*. His stomach heaved. Not that beautiful boy who'd just learned to walk. The son Dean had been so proud of and whom Gloria had smothered with affection.

"Alex?"

He doubled over, clamping a hand over his mouth and trying not to gag.

Tammy moved closer to his side. "I hear something, Alex."

He glanced up. Tears marred her smooth cheeks,

mingling with the dirt and rain on her face. "They're gone," he choked. "There's no one."

"No." She shook her head. "Listen."

Alex heard it then. A faint cry, no louder than a weak whisper, swept by his ear on a surge of wind. He couldn't tell if it was an animal or a human. If it was a final cry of death or a declaration of life. All he knew as he scanned the wreckage in front of him was that he was terrified of what he might find.

Chapter Two

Tammy tilted her head and strained to pinpoint the soft cries escaping the demolished house in front of her. They were muffled and seemed to emanate from a stack of rubble next to…

She stifled a sob, tore her eyes from the couple lying in front of her and pointed at a high pile of debris. "There," she said.

For a moment, she didn't think Alex would move. He remained doubled over beside her, silent and still. But when a fresh round of cries rang out from the rubble, he shot upright, scrambled toward the towering mass in the center of the demolished home and began heaving jagged two-by-fours out of the way.

The broad muscles of his back strained the thin, wet material of his T-shirt as he flung the debris away. He jerked to a stop when he reached a ragged portion of a wall—the only one left standing. A battered door dangled from its hinges and barely covered an opening.

Tammy stepped to his side, hope welling within her chest. Other than a hole having been punched through the upper corner, the door looked relatively untouched. Just like the plastic hanger sitting on the ground in front of it. And the healthy cry of a child reverberated within.

Alex reached out and gripped the doorknob, the shine of the brass dulled by mud and bits of leaves. The door squeaked as he pulled it out slowly, then propped it open. The dim light from the cloudy sky overhead barely lit the interior.

A young child huddled on the ground against the back corner. He stopped crying and looked up, his red cheeks wet with tears. The denim overalls and striped shirt he wore were damp, too.

His big brown eyes moved from Tammy to Alex, then his face crumpled. A renewed round of cries escaped him and echoed over the ravaged landscape surrounding them. Chubby hands reached up toward Alex, the small fingers grasping empty air.

Tammy gasped, her chest burning, and glanced at Alex.

He didn't move. He stood motionless amid thick planks of wood and pink insulation. The increasing gusts of wind ruffled his hair and a stoic expression blanketed his pale face.

"Alex?"

Throat aching, Tammy hesitated briefly, then knelt and scooped up the boy. His thin arms wrapped tight around her neck, and his hot face pressed against her skin, his sobs ringing in her ears.

"Alex." She spoke firmly and dipped her head toward the boy at her chest. "What's his name?"

Alex blinked, eyes refocusing on her, and whispered, "Brody."

Tammy smoothed a palm gently over the boy's soft brown hair. "We're here, Brody." Her chin trembled, and she bit her lip hard before saying, "We're here now."

She stepped carefully over a large portion of the roof,

the tattered shingles flapping in the wind and clacking against the rafters.

"Don't let him see," Alex rasped.

He moved swiftly to block the couple behind them, then cleared a safe path to the grass.

Tammy walked slowly behind him, swallowing hard and concentrating on his confident movements. His brawny frame seemed massive above the razed house, and under normal circumstances his towering presence would have set her nerves on edge. But she didn't feel the usual waves of apprehension. Only a deep sense of gratitude. And she found herself huddling closer to his back with each step, the boy in her arms growing quiet by the time they'd reached the road.

Alex stopped and held out his hands, slight tremors jerking his fingers. "Let me have him."

Tammy nodded and eased Brody into his arms. Alex squatted, set Brody on his feet, then ran his palms over the boy's limbs. He examined him closely.

"Nothing's broken," he said, his strained voice tinged with wonder. "There's not a scratch on him."

Brody whimpered and took two clumsy steps forward, bumping awkwardly between Alex's knees and settling against his broad chest. He laid his head against Alex's shirt and gripped the material with both hands.

"I know, little man." Alex dropped a swift kiss to the top of Brody's head before pressing him back into Tammy's arms. He spun away and started walking. "We better get him to the house. More clouds are rolling in."

Tammy looked up, her lids fluttering against the sporadic drizzle falling from a darker sky, then followed Alex. They took a different path than before, moving farther up the road before crossing to avoid the downed power line. The dirt drive leading to Alex's house had transformed to slick mud, and what was left of the late-afternoon light died, giving way to night and leaving the ravaged path cloaked in darkness.

Tammy swiped a clammy hand over her brow when they finally reached the front lawn. It seemed like the longest walk she'd ever taken. Her arms grew heavy with Brody's weight as she waited outside for Alex to check the house and make sure it was structurally sound.

"Razz," she called softly, cradling Brody's head against the painful throb in her chest and peering into the darkness.

Closing her eyes, she shifted the baby to her other hip and listened for the sound of hooves or neighs but heard neither. Only the rhythmic chirp of crickets, the faint croak of frogs and a sprinkle of rain striking the ground filled the empty land surrounding them.

Her legs grew weak, and a strange buzzing took over, assaulting her senses and mingling with the re-membered images of Brody's parents lying among the rubble.

"You can come in." Alex stood on the front porch, holding a camping lantern. The bright light bathed his handsome features and highlighted the weather-beaten foliage littering the steps below him. "It's safe. Just be careful of the glass."

Safe. Tammy pulled in a strong breath and held Brody tighter as she made her way inside. She hadn't felt that way in a long time. Not a single corner of the world felt safe anymore, and she never stayed in one place long enough to find out if it was.

"We should probably get him out of those wet

clothes." Alex gestured toward the dark hallway and turned to close the door behind them.

The door frame had been damaged by the storm, and he kicked the corner of it with his boot repeatedly until it shut. Tammy walked slowly down the hall, feeling her way with a hand on the wall as they drifted out of reach of the lantern's light and arrived at the first door on the left. She fumbled around to find the doorknob, then twisted, but it was locked.

"Not there," he bit out.

She jumped and glanced over her shoulder. Brody lifted his head from her chest and started crying again.

Alex winced and looked down, cursing softly. "I'm sorry," he said, easing awkwardly around them and moving farther down the hall. "I don't use that room. And the windows are blown out in the guest room." He opened a door at the end of the hall and motioned for her to precede him inside. "But you're welcome to this one."

She took a few steps, then hesitated at the threshold, an uneasy feeling knotting in her stomach as she scrutinized his expression. He'd sheltered her during intense events, and she truly believed she'd seen him at one of his weakest moments back at the demolished home. But…he was still a stranger. One who obviously cared for Brody but refused to hold the boy. And she'd learned a long time ago that a kind face could mask a multitude of evils.

Alex slowly reached out and rubbed his hand over Brody's back. "I'm sorry," he repeated gently. "From the looks of your truck, you're not going to be able to drive it tonight. Power's out. Landlines and cell service are down, so we can't make any calls, either. I did mean what I said. You're welcome to use this room tonight."

His expression softened, and his tempting mouth curved up at the corners in what she suspected was supposed to be a smile. But it fell flat, as though he rarely used it, and he turned away.

Broken. Tammy swallowed hard past the lump in her throat. His body was agile, solid and strong. But his smile was broken.

She straightened and followed him into the room, trying to shake off the strange thought—and the unfamiliar urge to touch him. To comfort a man. They both arose from the intensity of the day's events. And the loss he and Brody had suffered was enough to evoke sympathy from even the hardest of hearts.

"I pull from a well, so there's no running water." Alex crossed the room and riffled through the closet. Hangers clacked, and clothing rustled. "I have some bottled water on hand that I can put in the bathroom for you." He held up a couple of shirts and a pair of jogging pants. "It wouldn't hurt for you to put on some dry clothes, too. These will swallow you both whole, but they'll at least keep you comfortable while the others dry out."

Tammy looked down and plucked at her soggy T-shirt and jeans. Brody squirmed against her, squinting against the light Alex held.

"I'll wait in the kitchen," Alex said. "If you don't mind seeing to Brody?"

At her nod, he placed the clothes and lantern on a dresser, then left, calling over his shoulder, "I'll take the wet clothes when you're done and lay 'em out to dry."

"Thank you," she said.

But he was gone.

The white light glowing from the lantern lit up half of

what seemed to be the master bedroom, and the dresser cast a long shadow over an open door on the other side of the bed. The room definitely belonged to Alex. If the absence of feminine decor hadn't hinted strongly enough, the light scent of sandalwood and man—the same one that had enveloped her as Alex had covered her in the hallway—affirmed it.

Brody made a sound of frustration and rubbed his face against the base of her throat.

"Guess it's just you and me for now." She cradled him closer, closed the door, then grabbed the lantern from the dresser. "Let's get cleaned up, okay?"

It took several minutes to gather what she needed from the bathroom and strip the wet clothes from Brody. He grew fussy, wriggling and batting at her hands as he lay on a soft towel on the bed.

"Mama." He twisted away from her touch and tears rolled down his cheeks. "Mama."

"I know, baby," Tammy said, scooting closer across the mattress. "I'm so sorry." She strained to keep her voice steady and forced herself to continue. "I'll be quick, I promise."

She hummed a soft tune while she worked, hesitating briefly after removing the diaper and cleaning his bottom, then grabbed one of the T-shirts Alex had provided.

"This will have to do for now," she said, folding the cotton shirt into a makeshift diaper around him and tying knots at the corners. "I'll get something better soon."

He rubbed his eyes with a fist, and his thumb drifted toward his mouth. Tammy caught it before it could slip between his lips, then wiped it clean with a damp washcloth. His face scrunched up, and he fussed until she released it.

"There," she whispered, bending close and placing her palm to the soft skin of his chest. His heart pulsated beneath her fingertips. "Does that feel a little better?"

Brody blinked slowly, his eyes growing heavy as they wandered over her face. He returned his thumb to his mouth, and his free hand reached up, his fingers tangling in her hair, rubbing the damp strands. He grew quiet, drifted off, and his hand slipped from her hair to drop back to the mattress.

A heavy ache settled over Tammy and lodged in her bones. Being careful not to wake him, she stood and gathered several towels from the bathroom. She rolled each one and arranged them on the bed around him as a barrier.

Keeping a close eye on him, she changed out of her wet clothes and into the dry ones Alex had provided. Her mouth quirked as she held the jogging pants to her middle to keep them from falling. Alex had been right. The pants were at least three sizes too big, but she folded the waistband over several times and tied a knot in the bottom of the T-shirt to take up some of the slack in both.

When she was finished, she pulled her cell phone from the soggy pocket of her jeans and tried calling Jen. But there was no service, just as Alex had said. Sighing, she turned it off, gathered up the wet clothes and lantern, then made her way down the hall, drawing to an abrupt halt in the kitchen.

Alex stood by the sink, tossing back a shot glass and drinking deeply. He stilled as the light bathed his face and the bottle of whiskey in his hand.

A trickle of dread crept across the flesh of her back and sent a chill up her neck. The sight was nothing new. Her father had adopted the same pose every morning and every night. For him, each day began and ended with a bottle, and she imagined it was still that way, though she hadn't laid eyes on him in eight years.

The desire to run was strong. It spiked up her legs and throbbed in her muscles, urging her to drop everything and take off. Even if it meant walking twenty miles in the dark to the nearest town.

"I brought the wet clothes," Tammy said, shifting from one foot to the other, her boots crunching over shards of broken glass. "I can lay them out if you'll just tell me where—"

"No." He set the shot glass and bottle on the counter, then held out his hand. It still trembled, and the light from the lantern couldn't dispel the sad shadows in his eyes. "I'll take care of them. Thanks."

The calm tone of his voice eased her tension slightly, and she handed the clothes over before returning to the bedroom to check on Brody. She set the lantern on the nightstand, then trailed a hand over his rosy cheek, closing her eyes and focusing on his slow breaths.

His soft baby scent mingled with that of Alex's, still lingering on the sheets. Uncomfortable, she kissed Brody's forehead gently, then slipped away and stood by the window. She parted the curtains, and the glow from the lantern highlighted her reflection in the windowpane.

"He sleeping?"

Alex's broad chest appeared in the reflection behind her, and she stepped quickly to the side and faced him. "Yeah."

"Thanks for seeing to him," he said, looking at Brody.

Tammy nodded. "He...he's been asking for his mama."

He watched the baby, his mouth tightening, then took her place at the window. A muscle ticked in his strong jaw as he stared at the darkness outside.

Tammy fiddled with the T-shirt knotted at her waist. "I'm sorry about Dean and Gloria."

Alex dipped his head briefly, then turned away, shoving his hands in his pockets.

"Did you know them well?" she asked.

"Yeah." He dragged a broad hand over the back of his neck, his tone husky. "We all grew up together. Dean and I've been best friends since second grade. And Gloria and Susan—" His words broke off, and his knuckles turned white, his grip tightening around the base of his neck. "Dean helped me build this house. And I helped him build his."

Tammy stilled, her palms aching to reach out and settle over his hard grip. Ease the pain in some small way. She focused on his words instead, wondering who Susan was and why he'd clammed up so abruptly after mentioning her.

His wife, maybe? This was a big house for a single man. But she hadn't seen any women's clothing in the closet or feminine toiletries in the bathroom.

"Is Susan—"

A steady pounding drummed the roof and bore down on the walls of the house. Fat drops of water splattered against the windowpane, and steady streams began flowing down the glass.

"It's raining again," he said, releasing his neck and

placing his palm to the window. His biceps flexed below the soggy sleeve of his shirt. "I don't know when emergency services will make their rounds out here. We're so far from town." His whole body shook as he stared straight ahead. "I can't leave them out there alone," he choked. "Not like that."

He shoved off the window and strode swiftly to the door.

"Alex?"

He paused, gripping the door frame and keeping his broad back to her.

Tammy blinked back tears and gnawed her lower lip, wanting so much to help but feeling useless. "What can I do?"

He glanced over his shoulder, his voice thin. "Stay here and take care of Brody until I get back?"

She nodded. "Of course."

He left and the rain grew heavier, the sound of water pummeling the house filling the room. Rhythmic tings and plops started in the hallway as water leaked from the ceiling and hit the hardwood floor.

Shivering despite the heat of the summer night, Tammy moved slowly to the bed and sat down. She watched the empty doorway for over an hour, waiting to see if someone who knew Alex would walk in. A wife or girlfriend. Maybe a family member or friend. Anyone who cared enough to brave the weather, make the drive to Alex's ranch and check on him.

But no one did.

Eventually, the day became too heavy to carry, and the tears she'd struggled to hold back ran down her cheeks, the salty taste seeping into the corners of her mouth. She gave in and lay on the bed, curling into a ball near Brody and placing a comforting hand on his small shoulder.

She thought of Brody's parents and Razz in the dark, in the rain. She thought of Brody. And Alex…

His distinctive scent grew stronger as she silenced her sobs in the pillow and realized that, for the first time, she'd found two people who were more alone than she was.

"I'M REAL SORRY, ALEX."

Alex forced a nod as Jaxon Lennox, a paramedic and old classmate from high school, joined his colleague and lifted a second gurney into the back of an ambulance. The white sheet covering Dean flapped in the early-morning breeze.

Stomach churning, Alex spun away from the sight and studied the ruins of Dean's house. The rain from last night had soaked the wreckage, leaving deep puddles of dingy water on the piles of broken wood and battered bricks.

Alex had remained at Dean and Gloria's side all night until emergency services arrived in the early-morning hours. He'd been unable to bring himself to leave. The scene blurred in front of him, and he blinked hard, balling his fists against his thighs to keep from dragging them over his burning eyes.

The ambulance doors thudded closed, and Alex stiffened as footsteps approached from behind.

"I spoke to the sheriff. He said he'd contact a social worker this morning about the baby," Jaxon said. "Probably Ms. Maxine."

Alex held his breath and tried to suppress the heat welling in his chest and searing his cheeks. Deer Creek was a tiny community by anyone's standards, and everyone knew Ms. Maxine. Most everyone also knew Ms. Maxine had served as Alex's social worker from the time he'd turned five until he'd aged out of foster care at eighteen. She'd attended his high school graduation and his wedding. And had been the first guest at his and Susan's housewarming party eleven years ago, with an armful of gifts in tow.

Ms. Maxine was one of the brightest spots of a naively hopeful past that he wanted to forget.

"Sheriff said she should be at your place this afternoon to collect the child. I told him about that overturned truck at your place, too, and he said he'll send someone out as soon as he can." Jaxon sighed. "Wish we could've gotten here sooner, but things are so crazy right now. That storm was a monster, and it damaged a lot of houses, though this was the worst I've seen so far. Listen, I know you and Dean were close, and if you need anything…" His voice trailed away. "Well, you know where I am."

"Thanks," Alex said, barely shoving the word past his lips.

It'd be more polite to turn around and offer his hand or try to dredge up a smile, but he couldn't manage either. The expression of pity on a person's face was something he'd become unable to stomach.

The heavy presence at Alex's back disappeared, then a second set of doors slammed shut. An engine cranked, and the ambulance drove away, sloshing through the deep mudholes left in the dirt driveway of Dean's property.

Alex stared blindly at the rubble before him, frowning as the sun cleared the horizon. It blazed bright, tingeing the scoured landscape in a golden glow and coaxing the birds to sing in ravaged trees. There wasn't a single cloud marring the deep blue of the sky.

His skin warmed, and his soggy shirt and jeans clung uncomfortably to him. The damp band of his Stetson began to dry against his forehead, turning tight and stiff.

It was a hell of a thing—the sun rising on a day like this. The damned thing shouldn't have the nerve.

He scoffed and shook his head, squeezing his eyes hard enough to clear them, then started sifting through the mess on the ground for anything worth saving. A dented microwave, filled with muddy water, was lodged between broken staircase rails and a cracked cabinet door. Two recliners and one sofa were overturned, and the cushions were twisted within a tangle of curtains, sheets and wood beams. The remnants of a smashed crib littered a large, heavy pile of broken bricks.

Alex flinched, his boots jerking to a stop. This shouldn't have happened. Dean had walked the line all his life, married a good woman and had a healthy baby boy. This house should still be standing with their small family safely in it.

"I'm sorry, Dean," Alex said, plucking a bent nail from the ground and cringing at the tremor in his voice. "I should've built it stronger."

He gritted his teeth, flung the nail into the distance and kept moving, carefully investigating each stack of wreckage and methodically collecting the few scattered remains that might be of use. He shoved a few unbroken jars of baby food, several intact juice boxes and a half dozen dry disposable diapers into a stray trash bag. One hour later, he started back to his ranch, wanting nothing more than to guzzle a bottle of whiskey, collapse onto his bed and escape into oblivion.

But that wasn't a possibility. A woman and baby were still on his ranch—whatever little there was left of it—and he had to remain hospitable for at least a few more hours. Then they'd both be on their way and he'd have the comforting silence of privacy back.

The thought should've been a welcome one. But the relief he felt at their expected absence was overshadowed by a pang of loss. One that was accompanied by the warm image of Tammy's bright green eyes and the remembered feel of Brody's small, grasping fingers against his chest. All of which were ridiculous things for a man like him to dwell on.

Shrugging off the unwanted sensation, Alex picked up his pace and searched each empty field he passed for any sign of his horses. He'd made it past the downed power line and across the road when a sporadic pattering sounded behind him. It continued with each of his swift strides, then stopped abruptly when he stilled, a soft whine emerging at his back.

He glanced over his shoulder. A puppy—Labrador, maybe?—stood frozen in place, his yellow fur dark with mud and grime. The dog's black eyes widened soulfully, then he ducked his head and took up whining again.

Alex turned, then eased his bag to the ground. "Where'd you come from?"

The pup wagged his tail rapidly, then rolled belly up and wiggled. The leaves clinging to his matted fur and the pine needles stuck to his paws were an indication that he might have spent the night in the woods.

Alex lowered to his haunches and rubbed a hand over the puppy's thick middle before checking the rest of him for injuries. The dog was healthy, unharmed and looked to be about seven or eight weeks old.

"You belong to Earl, buddy?" he asked, scratching behind the pup's ear.

Old Earl Haggert bred and sold Labs. Could be one of his. Earl's place was about a mile up the road, and it was possible the dog might've wandered that far. With the storm they'd had yesterday, it seemed like everything had been displaced.

The dog stopped whining, licked Alex's fingers and nuzzled a wet nose into his palm.

Alex grinned, a soothing heat unfurling in his veins. "Well, hell. What's one more?" He stood, picked up his bag and started walking again. "You might as well come on." He patted his thigh with his free hand. "You can stay today, and I'll get you back to Earl tomorrow."

The dog followed, bounding forward with as much gusto as his short legs would allow.

"But it's only fair I warn you that there's not much to my place anymore." Alex slowed his step until the pup fell into a comfortable pace at his side. "Not after that tornado. My stable is shot, the fences are busted and my horses are missing. Got a damaged roof and broken windows all over the house. 'Bout the only thing not ruined was my bed, and a woman and baby are piled up on that."

The dog yelped up at him, and Alex cocked an eyebrow.

"I know, right? Only thing worse than all that is a man talking to himself." He grimaced, gripped the bag tighter and increased his pace again. "That's a damned shame in itself."

Alex clamped his mouth shut and forged ahead.

Rhythmic thuds echoed across the ravaged field as they drew closer to his house. He stopped a few feet from the end of the driveway, the dog skittering to an awkward halt against his shins.

Tammy pushed a wheelbarrow from one side of the front lawn to the other, pausing every few feet to pick up a broken tree limb and toss it into the cart. The wheels squeaked with each shove, and the contents clanged every time it bumped over uneven ground. Brody tottered close at Tammy's side, his brown hair gleaming in the sun. He followed her lead, bent to grab a stick and stumbled.

"Whoa, there." Tammy stopped the wheelbarrow and steadied him with one hand. She waited as he fumbled around in the grass, then straightened and held out a twig. "Good job," she praised, pointing at the wheelbarrow. "Can you put it in the cart?"

Brody stretched up on his tiptoes, flung the wood into the wheelbarrow and squealed.

"Nicely done," Tammy said, clapping.

Brody smiled, smacked his hands together awkwardly, then waddled toward another stick. Tammy laughed, her face lighting with pleasure.

The rich sound traveled across the front lawn and vibrated around Alex, sending a pleasurable tingle over his skin. He tried not to stare as she chased after Brody, her long brown hair falling in tangled waves over her shoulders and her slim legs moving with grace. They wore their clothes from last night and, though dry, her jeans and Brody's overalls were wrinkled and stained with mud.

But even weather-beaten, she and Brody were a beautiful sight. The kind he'd imagined years ago when he'd hammered shingles onto his newly constructed roof and set the windows in their frames. He'd spent the last free hour before his wedding looking through the glass pane of the kitchen window at the front lawn, envisioning Susan and the children they'd planned to have playing, laughing and living well.

Tammy's and Brody's energetic movements across the green grass breathed a bit of life into that old fantasy, conjuring it to the forefront of his mind and coaxing it past the tight knot in his chest. And it stung just as much as it soothed.

Alex averted his eyes and scrubbed the toe of his boot over the dirt.

"Hey."

He glanced up at the sound of Tammy's voice. She'd stopped following Brody and studied him closely, her gaze traveling over his face.

"I found the wheelbarrow out back and thought I'd make myself useful," she said, tucking her hair behind her ears and brushing a hand over her rumpled T-shirt. "Brody's been crying for his parents. I thought taking him outside and keeping him busy might help. Hope you don't mind. And I found a banana and cereal in the kitchen that I gave to him. The paramedics stopped by a couple of hours ago, and I sent them in your direction. Did they make it to you okay?"

He nodded, swallowing the thick lump in his throat, and gestured to the white bandage covering her temple. "How's your cut?"

Her fingers drifted up and touched it as though she'd forgotten it was there. "Oh, it's fine. I told them it was nothing, but they insisted on patching me up anyway." She waved a hand in the air, then shoved it in her pocket.

"They checked Brody out, too, while they were here. He's just like you said. Not a scratch on him."

Brody stood behind her, holding a stick out with a chubby hand and staring at the dog snuffling around in the dirt at Alex's heels. The boy's eyebrows rose, and his mouth parted. He pointed his free hand at the pup and shouted.

The dog poked his head between Alex's ankles. He eyed Brody, then bounded across the grass and leaped for the stick Brody held, knocking the boy down in the process.

Brody plopped down on his backside and sat, stunned, for a moment. His brown eyes widened and a wounded expression crossed his face before he took up crying.

Alex froze, a strangled laugh dying in his throat and escaping him in a choked grunt. Years ago, he'd seen Dean hit his butt in the same position with an identical look on his face. Except Dean had been twelve years old and the cause of it had been the kickback from a shotgun. One he'd swiped from his dad's gun cabinet and used without permission, accidentally shooting out a window on his dad's truck.

Dean had insisted he'd outgrown his BB gun, but he hadn't been too grown to shed tears that day. He'd taken one look at that shattered glass and cried, "My dad's gonna kick my ass good for this one!"

Of course, his dad hadn't. He'd fussed a great deal but had been relieved that Dean and Alex hadn't been injured. That they'd emerged from what could've been a deadly incident without a scratch on them. Like Brody.

A boy who would grow up without ever knowing how great a man his father had been.

Alex dropped his bag, turned his back on the trio and stifled a guttural roar, the rage streaking through him almost uncontainable.

"Oh, it's all right, Brody." Tammy's soothing words quieted the baby's sobs. "You're okay, and there are a lot more sticks where that one came from." There were shuffling sounds, then she asked, "This little guy a friend of yours, Alex?"

He glanced over his shoulder to find her kneeling on the ground, petting the dog and hugging Brody to her side. Her eyes met his, and the smile on her face melted away, a concerned expression taking its place. The kind he knew all too well.

Unable to answer her, he spun away, stalked up the front porch steps and entered the kitchen. He went straight to the cabinet, grabbed a bottle, then upended it, drinking deeply. The fiery liquid burned a trail down his throat and lit up his gut, forcing him to set it down and gasp for breath.

He watched through the window as Tammy got to her feet and took a hesitant step toward the house. She stopped, frowned up at the front porch, then walked away. The squeak of wheels rang out and the consistent clang of sticks being thrown into the cart resumed.

Alex gripped the edge of the counter and closed his eyes. She probably thought he was a crazy, selfish bastard. And to a certain extent he was. But how could he explain it? How could anything he might say help her understand?

He was truly grateful that Brody had survived the storm and that Tammy had escaped without serious injury. Last night as he'd grieved at Dean's side, he'd even thanked heaven that he, himself, had managed to emerge from yesterday's carnage still breathing. That he wasn't buried beneath the broken walls of his house being pummeled by rain.

But no amount of gratitude would ease the anger of knowing that death had stolen Dean and Gloria. Or change the fact that, sometimes, life could hurt like hell.

Chapter Three

A body rests easier after doing the right thing.

Alex stood on the front porch and waited as Tammy finished changing Brody's diaper on the grass, recalling the words Ms. Maxine had repeated to him a thousand times over the years. Ones she'd spoken when he'd gotten suspended from middle school for smoking, then reminded him of when he'd returned to his foster parents' house after sneaking out for a weekend party binge as a teen.

It was a phrase he'd grown to know well. And one he'd strictly adhered to after mending his ways and proposing to Susan.

But there were some things a man couldn't control.

He adjusted the bag of cookies under his arm and gripped the can of soda in his hand tighter, hoping the toothpaste he'd rubbed over his teeth masked the whiskey on his breath. Abstaining from the bottle between the hours of five in the morning and nine at night was a rule he'd taken pride in for nine years. But, surely, his grief from losing his best friends excused today's slip.

Only, his shortcomings were easier to deal with—and accept—when there were no witnesses to them.

Alex winced and rolled his shoulders to ease the tight

knot at the base of his neck. He couldn't stay holed up in the kitchen all afternoon, tossing back shots, while Tammy cleaned up the front yard and took care of Brody. The only thing left to do was pull his shit together and at least be hospitable. It was what any gentleman would do. And he still knew how to be one. Even if it'd been years since he'd put his good manners into practice.

A little longer. That's it. Make them comfortable for a few more hours, and soon Ms. Maxine would whisk Brody away to a new home and the wrecker would cart Tammy and her overturned truck back to the highway. Then he could curl up with a bottle for hours and grieve in private.

Alex nodded curtly and eased his way down the front steps to Tammy's side. "Figured you might be thirsty," he said, handing the soda to her as she knelt next to the baby. "Power's still out, so it's warm. Sorry about that."

"Thanks." She lifted Brody to his feet, then took the soda and popped the top.

Her slim throat moved as she drank deeply, drawing Alex's eyes to the flushed skin of her neck and upper chest. The dog climbed onto her knees and jumped to lick the can. She pushed him away with her free hand, causing the collar of her T-shirt to slip to one side. It revealed a faint tan line below her collarbones that contrasted sharply with the ivory complexion of the upper swell of her breast.

Alex had a sudden urge to trail his lips across her warm skin and breathe in her sweet scent. He peeled his gaze away, ignoring the heat simmering in his veins, and caught her eyes on him. She lowered the can, straightened her shirt with her free hand and pushed to her feet.

Ah, hell. A gentleman didn't ogle a woman, and this was becoming a habit.

Cheeks burning, he cleared his throat and gestured to the trash bag on the ground nearby. "I see you found the diapers. There's some baby food and juice in there, too. Not a lot. But enough to get him through at least one more day."

Something tugged at his jeans, and a frustrated squeal erupted. He looked down, finding Brody attempting to climb up his leg, his small arm stretched out and tiny fingers grabbing for the bag of cookies under Alex's arm.

Tammy laughed. "I don't think he's interested in baby food. Looks like he'd much rather get a hold of those cookies."

A soft breeze ruffled Brody's hair, and the boy blinked wide, pleading eyes up at him. The brown strands and deep chestnut pools were the same shade as Dean's, and his small cries were impossible to resist.

Alex's chest constricted so tight he could barely breathe. "A social worker is coming for him," he rasped, reminding himself as much as informing Tammy. He handed a cookie to Brody, then smoothed his knuckles across the boy's soft cheek. "And someone's arranging to have your truck and trailer hauled to the body shop in town. Don't know how long it'll take to fix 'em, but power will probably be restored in town first. You'll have a better chance of reaching a friend or family member sooner there."

She nodded absently, and her gaze drifted to the empty

field behind him. "I looked for Razz this morning," she said softly. "I couldn't find her."

"Your horse?"

"Yeah." Those emerald eyes returned to his face. "Do you think she survived?"

He grimaced, then watched Brody mouth the cookie and spin in awkward circles to avoid the puppy leaping for the treat. "Can't say for sure."

Chances were, her horse was gone along with all of his. God help him, he didn't want to lie to her. But he didn't want to see pain engulf those beautiful features, either.

"She might've made it," Alex said, squinting against the sharp rays of the sun and scanning the landscape. "There's a chance she's huddled up somewhere with mine."

Though he wouldn't bet what little money he had left on it. And he didn't even want to think about how much it'd cost to put this struggling ranch back in working order.

"How many do you have?" she asked.

"Ten."

"You board them?"

"And breed them." He turned to study a field behind him. "Mainly for ranch work. I try for blue roans, since they've brought in the most over the past two years." His throat tightened. "Dean was my partner."

Brody yelped and reached for a second cookie. Alex gave him another, then held the bag out to Tammy. She took a cookie and turned it over in her hand, staring at it with a furrowed brow.

"I know the storm was bad," she said. "But Razz is

fast." She glanced up, a hesitant smile appearing. "She's the best barrel horse on the circuit."

So, she raced. Alex surveyed the slim but strong curves of Tammy's arms and legs more closely. No wonder she'd held her own through yesterday's nightmare. The few rodeo riders he'd known were a tough lot. Full of grit and fight.

He'd never taken to the circuit life, though he'd tried it once years ago, riding bulls one summer in his early twenties. It was fun, brought in a decent amount of cash and provided an outlet for his reckless streak. But then he'd started missing Susan and realized he wanted her more. Wanted a wife and home. A family of his own. And he'd decided it wasn't fair to keep Susan waiting. That he should return to Deer Creek, settle down like Dean and do the right thing.

His jaw clenched. If he'd known then how much he'd end up disappointing Susan, the right thing to do would've been a very different choice.

"I'm hoping she dodged the worst of it."

Alex blinked and refocused on Tammy's face, his stomach dropping. "What?"

"Razz," Tammy clarified, studying him again. "She might have outrun the tornado, and if she managed to survive, then maybe your horses did, too." Her attention drifted to Brody, and her smile widened. "After all, this little guy came out of it okay."

Brody grinned, his mouth laden with crumbs, and stretched his arms out to Tammy. She slipped her cookie in her pocket, lifted him up and cradled his head against her chest.

"Yeah, he did," Alex murmured, his eyes clinging to

the gentle embrace of her arms around Brody and the slow sway of her body as she rocked him.

The movements were calming, and Brody soaked it up, his eyelids growing heavy and his breaths slowing. Her brown hair slipped over her shoulder and rested against Brody, the wavy locks sharing the same chestnut tones as those of the baby.

She was a natural at comforting a child and, had Alex not known better, he would have assumed Brody belonged to her. It would be the easiest thing in the world to mistake the two of them for family. For mother and son.

An ache streamed through Alex's limbs, making his palms itch to reach out and tug them both close. To hold them in a protective embrace, feel the steady pulse of their hearts and draw strength from their solid presence. To imagine, just for a moment, that he belonged, too. As a man and a father...

But that would be a mistake. He stiffened and turned away. He'd been abandoned as a child and had struggled to fit in with each of the three foster families he'd lived with as a youth. He'd had to fight his damnedest to establish enough stability in his life to offer Susan the promise of a secure future filled with family and happiness. Things he'd failed to deliver, wrecking Susan's dreams along with his own.

No. Nature knew what it was doing. He wasn't built to be a family man—it wasn't in his DNA to be a father—and he was foolish for even entertaining the fantasy.

"Someone's here."

Tammy's words were joined with the faint churn of an engine and the slosh of tires through mud down the driveway. A compact car eased over the hill, maneuvered around various piles of debris and drew to a stop several feet behind the fallen tree blocking the path. The door opened, and an older woman stepped out, wisps of gray hair escaping her topknot in the soft breeze.

Alex caught his breath, smothering the urge to run into her arms and seek comfort like he had as a boy. Instead, he placed the bag of cookies on the ground, took off his hat and waited.

A sad smile dispersed the soft wrinkles lining the woman's face as she made her way over. "Oh, Alex." She wrapped her arms tight around him, standing on the toes of her high heels to whisper in his ear, "I'm so sorry about Dean and Gloria."

A low cry dislodged from Alex's throat and pried its way out of his mouth. He coughed, closing his throat against another sob, and tucked the top of her head gently under his chin. "Thank you, Ms. Maxine."

He gave in to the moment, closing his eyes and squeezing her close. The familiar scent of her perfume arose from her clothing, and the sweet aroma took him back years. All the way back to when he was a dumb kid and the only bright spot in each day had been her forgiving smile and unconditional support. Ms. Maxine was the closest he'd ever come to having a real mother. His mother had abandoned him at an early age. And from what little information Maxine had available to share with him, his father had never been in the picture.

"I'm so thankful that you're okay." Maxine pulled back and cupped his face with her palms as she scrutinized him. "I think a shave, a wholesome meal and a good night's rest are in order." She smiled. Bright and sincere. "Though even without that, I think you're more handsome now than you were the last time I saw you."

He ducked his head, his neck and chest warming. It'd been years since he'd last seen her. Hurt and anger had knotted in his gut the day Susan left, and he'd pushed everyone away, including Maxine. He'd avoided her calls and visits. Had never been able to face the possibility of seeing disapproval in Maxine's eyes. But there wasn't a trace of disappointment in her expression.

Just sympathy and kindness.

Alex reached up, cradled her thin wrists gently in his hands and managed a small grin. "Nah. I've just gotten old."

"Old?" Maxine scoffed. "You've got years ahead of you before you qualify as being old." She chuckled, patted his cheeks, then gestured toward his hair. "No, my dear boy. You've just got a touch of silver fox in you."

The dog yelped and squirmed its way between them, his tail thumping against Alex's leg as he gnawed on the toe of his boot.

"Well, hello." Maxine bent and scratched the dog's head, then leaned to the side, her eyes straying to Tammy and Brody. "And who do we have here?"

Alex stepped to the side and swept an arm toward the pair. "Ms. Maxine, this is Tammy Jenkins. The tornado forced her off the road yesterday."

Maxine nodded toward the overturned truck and trailer on the other side of the driveway. "I see that. I'm Maxine Thompson and it's very nice to meet you, although I wish it were under different circumstances." She held out a hand, which Tammy shook. "I'm sorry about your truck, dear. But don't worry. The sheriff asked me to relay to Alex that he's arranging for it to be towed to Sam Bircham's shop. Sam's the best mechanic in town, and he'll have it as good as new before you know it. They're overwhelmed right now, though, and he asked me to let you know it'll be a while before he can get to it. If you need to send a message to a family member or friend, I'd be happy to pass it along to the sheriff when I return to town. He'll make sure it reaches them."

Tammy smiled, rearranging Brody on her hip as he straightened in her arms. "Thank you."

"And this must be our beautiful Brody." Maxine rubbed the baby's arm and sighed as he burrowed his face back into Tammy's chest. "What a sweet boy." Her voice lowered. "How's he doing?"

"As well as can be expected," Tammy said, kissing the top of Brody's head.

Maxine looked the pair over, then flashed a tender smile before saying, "I see he's taken to you, Tammy. It's so good of you to look after him during this difficult time."

Alex felt a small smile emerge on his own face, the pleased glow in Tammy's cheeks provoking it. She and Brody were such a beautiful sight.

"Oh, it's no trouble," Tammy said, blushing. "He's a joy."

Maxine made a sound of agreement, her eyes moving from Tammy to Alex and back again, then wrapped her hand around Alex's elbow. "Will you please excuse us for a minute?"

Tammy nodded, and Maxine tugged Alex several feet away to stand facing the field. The dog followed, bumped into the back of his leg, then started snuffling around the grass.

"How are you, Alex?" Maxine asked, peering up at him.

"Fine." Alex dodged her watchful eyes and gestured toward the field. "I'll be better if I manage to find my horses in good health and get the business going again. But without Dean…" He sucked in a strong breath and replaced his hat on his head. "I think this ranch may have reached the end of the line."

"Oh, I wouldn't say that." Maxine shifted at his side, her sleeve brushing his arm as she swiveled to survey the house and stable. "There may be some damage," she continued, facing him again, "but your foundation is strong. With time and a little elbow grease, this place will breathe again."

Alex's mouth tightened as he scanned the demolished fences, ravaged trees and barren paddocks. Ms. Maxine meant well. But that'd be a lot easier said than done.

"I worry about you," Maxine added softly. "Hiding out here all by yourself for so long."

"I'm not hiding—"

"Yes, you are." The firmness in her voice forced him to meet her eyes again, the blue depths earnest behind her glasses. "You're not a quitter, Alex. Never have been." She glanced at Tammy and Brody, then stepped closer to his side. "If I asked for a favor, would you humor me?" she asked. "For old times' and an old woman's sake?"

Alex stiffened, acutely aware of Tammy's curious stare and the dog chewing on the toe of his boot. "Depends."

"How long is Tammy staying?"

He shrugged. "Just till the wrecker gets here, I imagine. She's a barrel racer and is probably itching to get back on the circuit already."

Maxine sighed. "Dean didn't have a will, and I know he lost his father a few years ago. I've left messages for his half brother in Boston, but it may be a while before I hear back. Do you know of any family Gloria might've had that I could contact for Brody?"

Alex shook his head. "Not that I know of. Gloria's mother remarried and moved to California years ago. She was never big on keeping in touch. That's one reason why—"

He stilled his tongue. No need to drag Maxine through the mud he, Dean and Gloria had lived through in their lives and point out how it'd glued them together. Besides, nothing stayed a secret for long in Deer Creek, and he'd be willing to bet she already knew most of it anyway.

Maxine frowned. "Everything's a bit chaotic in town what with all the damage from the storm. If I take Brody now, I'll have to place him in a children's home near Atlanta until I'm able to find a suitable foster family. I can't bring myself to take Brody so far from home just yet. Not when there's a possibility of him being cared for by someone he already knows."

Alex stilled, an unpleasant prickling sensation snaking up the back of his neck. "What are you getting at?"

"Would you be willing to take Brody in until I can finalize a permanent placement for him?"

He held up a hand. "Ms. Maxine—"

"It wouldn't be for too long," she interjected. "Just for a little while. Brody's been through such a traumatic experience and he knows you."

"Yeah, he knows me," Alex sputtered, a stabbing pain ripping through him as an old wound reopened. His eyes flicked over Brody as he snuggled against Tammy's chest. "But that doesn't make me a fit guardian."

"It would only be temporary, and I'd be in this with

you. Judging from that overturned truck, that young lady's not leaving Deer Creek anytime soon. She'll need somewhere to stay. I know it's not good to assume..." Maxine hesitated, nodding pointedly in Tammy's direction. "But I think if you asked, you might get more help than you'd ordinarily expect."

The surprised expression on Tammy's face made it clear she'd heard every word. It also made Alex's heart slam rapidly against his ribs.

Open the door of his battered house and washed-up life to a baby and stranger?

"Hell, no," Alex muttered, stumbling back and shaking his boot to dislodge the pup. "And you're right about the assuming thing. When you assume, you make a pair of asses out of—"

"Language, Alex."

He bit his tongue. That was a familiar tone. Her no-nonsense one. "Sorry," he mumbled. "But it's a bad idea."

"If you won't do it for me, will you do it for Dean?" Maxine asked softly.

Alex winced, a hollow forming in his gut. Damn. She wasn't pulling any punches.

"I'm sorry, Alex. I wish none of this had happened," she whispered. "But it did. And, sometimes, the best way to take your mind off your own pain is to help alleviate someone else's. Please do this for Dean. And for Brody. It's just for a little while."

Alex dropped his head back and closed his eyes, flinching as the dog growled playfully and bit into his boot harder. "And what am I supposed to do with a baby and a woman?"

"Where the baby is concerned," Maxine said, "it'll come to you. As for the woman…"

At her prolonged silence, he opened his eyes and faced her. Her mouth stretched slowly into a grin.

"Well, as for the woman…" She winked. "If I have to explain that to you, you've been hiding out from civilization for longer than I thought."

A stifled laugh came from Tammy's direction.

Lord, help him. He spun on his heels and stalked off, the dog yipping and biting at the hem of his jeans along the way.

"Alex," Maxine called. "A body always rests easier after—"

"Doing the right thing," Alex grunted back, waving the words away with his hand.

Only, it was the damnedest thing. None of this felt right. None of it at all.

TAMMY SILENCED ANOTHER giggle with her hand, watching Maxine shake her head as Alex stomped off.

Good grief, she was being rude but couldn't help it. A constant stream of laughter bubbled in her belly at the sight of Alex stumbling over the small puppy at his feet, his muscular frame jerking awkwardly to avoid stepping on the animal.

"He barks a lot but never bites."

Tammy lowered her hand, still laughing. "What?"

Maxine chuckled, too, and walked over. "Alex. He may come across as a mean ol' grouch, but he's just a big teddy bear underneath. You just have to be patient enough to get past it all."

Tammy's laughter died out, and she shifted from one foot to the other as Maxine smiled at her. Her arms trembled beneath the weight of Brody's sleeping form, and the familiar trickle of trepidation crept into her veins. The other woman had a kind face and pleasant personality, but her wise eyes saw too much. And there were so many things Tammy didn't want anyone to ever see. Most especially, her constant fear of men. It made her feel weak and vulnerable.

"I see he's drifted off," Maxine murmured, smoothing a hand over Brody's back. She held her hands out, palms up. "Would you mind?"

Tammy shook her head. "No, not at all."

She passed Brody to Maxine, then helped settle him comfortably within her arms. Brody pulled in a noisy breath, then nuzzled his cheek against Maxine's neck as he settled back into sleep.

"He's so precious." Maxine kissed the top of his head, then grinned. "I hope you didn't mind me pushing you out on a limb earlier with Alex. I'm just hoping you might consider helping him out and tending to Brody while you wait for your truck to be repaired. You seem to be a natural with kids."

Tammy lifted a shoulder briefly, her belly warming. "Oh, I don't know. Brody is easy to love, and I've always wanted a houseful of children."

The smile on the other woman's face dimmed. "Do you have children, Tammy?"

"No. But someday…"

Tammy tensed, the words trailing away as she wondered for the millionth time how she'd ever have a family if she couldn't manage to trust a man.

"It's just me right now," Tammy added, shoving her hands in her pockets. "I was actually on the way to help my best friend with her wedding plans when the storm hit. She's getting married next month."

Maxine's face brightened. "Oh, how exciting. Weddings have always been my favorite event. Alex had a beautiful—" She stopped short, and her mouth flattened. "Well, that's not for me to discuss."

Tammy hesitated, sneaking a peek at Alex's broad back as he disappeared into the stable on the other side of the property. The dog scuttled in after him. "Is Alex married?"

Maxine looked down and rubbed small circles over Brody's back, her tone sad. "He was at one time. But not now."

Tammy dragged her teeth over her bottom lip. "Does he have any family?" She hurried to add, "I don't mean to pry, but I couldn't help but wonder when no one came to check on him last night."

The other woman nudged her glasses up with a knuckle and shook her head. "Alex has been alone a long time. That's one reason why he has trouble accommodating guests." She smiled. "But I think it'd do him good to have Brody around for a bit. It might help him get over losing Dean and allow him to find a bright spot in all of this." She hugged Brody, her expression lifting. "And this young man is definitely a bright spot."

Tammy laughed softly. "Yes, he is."

Maxine walked over to her car. "I brought some supplies for Brody and, once the news spread this morning, a few ladies from my church went to the Red Cross setup in town and fixed a few plates of food for y'all. It's nothing special but should get you through today and tomorrow. And, hopefully, power will be restored soon."

Maxine retrieved her keys and started to unlock the

trunk, but Tammy stalled her, saying, "Why don't you let me get that for you?"

"Thank you." Maxine handed over the keys. "There are three boxes, and they're rather heavy. You might want to ask Alex to lend you a hand. I'll take Brody inside." She headed toward the house. "Where should I set him down for a nap?"

"Alex let us use his room last night."

Maxine nodded, then made her way up the front porch, tossing over her shoulder, "Remember what I said about Alex. Don't let that grouchy facade fool you."

Tammy opened the trunk, then jingled the keys in her hand, listening to the birds chirp as her skin absorbed the warmth of the sun. A soft breeze whispered over the tall grass in the field, ruffled through her hair, then scattered leaves around on the front porch. Even with the visible damage from the storm, the grounds were peaceful and welcoming. She could only imagine how beautiful the ranch would be fixed up.

If she did manage to find Razz, the spacious fields would be a perfect place for the mare to spend a few calm days before returning to the circuit. Her stomach churned at the thought of leaving without knowing what happened to her racing partner. Even if the worst had happened, she'd rather know than not. And the thought of Alex struggling to restore his ranch and take care of Brody alone made her ache.

Staying would interfere with her plans to spend the month with Jen, but once she explained the situation, surely her best friend would understand. Plus, she couldn't go anywhere until her truck was fixed. According to Maxine's estimation, finding a placement for Brody would take two or three weeks at the most.

That would still leave one week to help Jen prepare for the wedding.

Decision made, Tammy shoved the keys in her pocket, shut the trunk and headed for the stable Alex had entered. The scent of honeysuckle lingered on the air and calmed her nerves, spurring her boots across the thick grass to the cool, shaded entrance. The steady pound of a hammer clanged from inside.

"Alex?"

She knocked on the wide door. Debris from the storm had battered the shine off the wood, and the hinges squeaked as she shoved it farther to the side. The pounding stopped, and the clicking of claws against hardwood rang out, echoing around the empty building as the puppy barreled around the corner.

"Hey, buddy." Tammy petted the dog, then went inside, scanning the line of stalls gracing opposite sides of the building.

It was a large structure by anyone's standards, built for forty horses with twenty stalls on either side. She nudged bits of broken wood and twisted metal out of the aisle with the toe of her boot. Scattered patches of sunlight dotted the littered floor, and she looked up, eyeing the jagged holes in the roof.

"Not a pretty sight, is it?"

She stopped. Alex emerged from a stall at the end of the aisle, carrying a set of broken stall bars, which he leaned against the wall.

"It needs some work," she said.

He grunted and rolled his thick shoulders. Dust clung to his jeans and T-shirt, casting a gray haze over his brawny build beneath the speckled sunlight. "That's an understatement."

"Maxine brought some supplies for Brody." Tammy watched the puppy lap water noisily from a metal bowl on the floor, then took a hesitant step forward. "I started thinking that her idea might not be such a bad one."

Alex took his hat off and hung it on a broken stall post. She caught herself focusing on the thick waves of his hair and the way the rich, dark strands contrasted with the dusting of silver. Her fingertips yearned to trail through them, and she balled her hands into fists at her sides to fight the urge.

"I mean, you saved my life," she continued. "The least I could do is stick around for a little while and help you in return."

He didn't answer. Or ask. Just turned his head and stared at the disarray of the stable.

"You'll need an extra hand with Brody around," she said. "I'm used to hard work, and I wouldn't mind taking care of Brody and helping out wherever I can. I could help you look for your horses, and hopefully we'll find Razz, too."

Alex looked at her then, his dark five o'clock shadow rippling as his jaw clenched. His eyes were haunted, and exhaustion lined his features.

Tammy rolled her lips and pressed them together hard, trying her best to ignore the flutter in her belly and the odd desire to move closer. To lean against the muscular wall of his chest and wrap her arms around him.

"You'd be doing me a favor, too, you know? If I do find Razz, she'll need a calm place to rest before I take her back out on the road. And I *will* find her. She's a strong horse, and I can't leave without at least knowing—" She cleared her throat and gestured toward the empty stalls. "I can help you get the stable back in working order in exchange for you boarding Razz for a while. Then, maybe by the time my truck is repaired, Brody will have a new home and Razz and I will move on. It's a win-win situation for us both."

A heavy sigh escaped him. "I guess you have a point," he said, approaching. "And a deal."

He held his hand out, the big, tanned palm tilted in an open invitation for hers.

Tammy tensed, a tight knot forming in her throat. *Teddy bear.* She uncurled her fist and rubbed her hand over her jeans, recalling Maxine's words. *He's just a big teddy bear.*

"Deal," she whispered, slipping her hand into his.

His palm was rough with calluses, but his long fingers wrapped around her hand, encompassing it in caressing warmth. He squeezed gently, and a delicious shiver of longing traveled through her. The kind of longing that made her want to slide her hand up his wrist, smooth her fingers over his thick biceps and cup his chiseled jaw. To see his tempting mouth stretch into a smile. A real one.

"Now you'll have to figure out what to do with me," she teased. "Seeing as how I'm just a woman and all."

His dark brows rose, and his mouth twitched. His lips parted, revealing white teeth and deep dimples. A low rumble escaped him, the sound rich and sincere. It swept through the hollow interior of the stable and the empty space within her, filling both with joy.

"It's not broken."

His laughter trailed away, confusion marring his features. "What?"

Tammy froze, realizing she'd voiced the thought aloud. "Your mouth," she mumbled. "I…I mean your smile. I thought it looked broken yesterday when…" She tugged her hand free of his, face burning as he stared at her. "It's nothing."

He watched her for a moment, then lowered his head and leaned in, stopping when she took a step back. His gray eyes traveled over her face, and that small spark of desire reignited within her. It rushed through her veins, prompting her to lift her chin and present her mouth in an invitation of her own.

Alex moved closer, his familiar scent surrounding her as his warm lips brushed softly across hers. Her eyes fluttered shut, and she breathed him in, savoring the tenderness of the moment. Wanting to hold on to it. Wanting, for the first time, to hold on to a man.

But the moment was over.

The heat of his presence faded, and her eyes sprang open.

"It's not broken, baby," he murmured, easing away. His relaxed expression vanished, and a frown took its place. "But a lot of other things are."

The dog whined and leaped at Tammy's knees, his small body banging against her shins. Seeking a distraction, she knelt on weak legs beside the puppy and stroked his soft fur. The rapid thump of her heart made her catch her breath and her fingers trembled. All sorts of emotions she'd never felt before swirled in her belly and swelled within her chest.

"It's not a good idea to get attached to that dog."

She looked up. Alex stood at the other end of the aisle, watching the pup.

His eyes shifted to her, and his voice softened. "Or Brody, for that matter. The wind that blew the three of you in here is gonna carry you all away just as fast in different directions."

Alex reentered the stall, and the steady pounding of a hammer resumed.

"Maybe," Tammy whispered. Her lips still tingled from his kiss, and she touched her fingertips to them, smiling as the puppy snuggled against her middle. "But we're here for now."

Chapter Four

Alex firmed his stance in the bed of his truck and swung the ax hard, grunting with satisfaction at the sharp crack of wood beneath it. The busted branch flopped to the side and slid off the back of the truck's tailgate to the ground. Each scrape of bark against metal left more scratches than the truck had already suffered, but prying the vehicle free and clearing the fallen tree from the driveway was more important.

He and Tammy had worked on it yesterday afternoon after Maxine had left, then resumed early this morning after searching for the horses, spending the majority of the day continuing their efforts. With no power and no sign of the horses, there wasn't much left to do but keep busy and hope for the best.

"I think it's safe to say you'll have enough firewood for the winter," Tammy said, looking up at him. She grabbed the thick end of the branch and dragged it off the driveway toward the large pile of limbs behind her. "Maybe three winters after you chop up the rest of the downed trees."

She dropped the branch, puffed a strand of hair out of her flushed face, then beat her gloved hands together. Dust billowed out, and she coughed, squinting against the low-hanging sun as she surveyed the fields before them.

Alex followed her gaze and cringed at the jagged line of broken trees on the other side of the grounds. It'd take at least a week to haul off all the fallen limbs. Hell, it'd taken all afternoon to chop up the few in the driveway, and they still weren't finished.

Though, he couldn't say Tammy hadn't pulled her weight. More than that. She'd chopped, heaved and hauled almost as much wood as he had today. And she hadn't complained once.

"Can we get it off the truck now?" Tammy asked, eyeing the tree trunk wedged over the tailgate in front of him. Sweat glistened on her forehead, and she dragged the back of her arm across it. "I know it's big, but we could tie a rope around it and with the two of us pulling—"

"No." Alex shook his head, his eyes drifting to the smooth curves of her lips. "It's too heavy for dragging and too thick for an ax. We'll need something stronger to cut it up first."

Her hopeful expression dimmed, and her mouth drooped, making him want to lean over, dip his head and place kisses at the corners. Coax and tease until they softened under his. Like yesterday...

Damn. He tossed the ax into the bed of the truck, swung his leg over the tailgate and hopped down. What the heck was wrong with him? Here he was, a grown man, fixating on a barely there kiss from hours ago with a woman he hardly knew. A woman he'd continued thinking about as he'd fought for sleep last night crammed on the living room couch while she and Brody occupied his bed.

But he guessed that was what nine years of self-imposed celibacy would do to a man. One touch of her soft palm against his made him ache to feel more. A chaste peck on the lips made him long to explore her mouth to see how sweet she tasted. And an entire day of working alongside her, her lithe movements brushing against him and her rapid breaths close to his ear, kept those unwelcome desires smoldering in his blood.

He jerked his gloves off, then scrubbed a hand over his face, the sharp scent of sap and pine invading his nostrils. It was just comfort his body was seeking. Something to take his mind off the fact that he'd no longer have Dean and Gloria in his life and how much that hurt.

The last thing he needed to do was get tangled up with a young barrel racer who'd hightail it back to the interstate in a couple weeks. No matter how much her long legs, soft curves and soul-searching eyes tempted him to—

Hell, he needed some space. Needed to stretch his legs, fill his lungs with fresh air and clear his head.

"No, Brody." Tammy tugged off the baggy gloves he'd loaned her and jogged across the driveway to the lawn.

Brody stood on one leg in the portable playpen Maxine had provided, holding on to the top edge and attempting to lift his other leg over it. The dog ran in circles around the structure and barked as the boy climbed. Each sharp yelp from the puppy prompted a frustrated wail from Brody.

"I know," Tammy soothed, lifting Brody out of the playpen and setting him on his feet. "That thing gets old after a while, doesn't it?"

The dog pounced playfully, springing into the air and nipping at the short sleeves of Brody's shirt. Tammy nudged him off, but the pup persisted, knocking into Brody's knees and causing the baby to stumble backward.

"'Bout time I take that dog back to its owner," Alex said, jumping at the chance to get away for a little while.

Tammy straightened the small baseball cap on Brody's head—another gift from Maxine—and pulled him closer to her side. "You know where he came from?"

"I've got a pretty good hunch. There's a man about a mile up the road that sells Labs. The dog probably wandered off from there. And he might have a chain saw I can borrow to break that tree up into manageable pieces." Alex threw his gloves onto the pile of wood, grabbed a flashlight from the glove box in his truck, then whistled to get the dog's attention. "Come on, boy. Let's go for a walk."

The dog joined him, and they made it three feet before Tammy called out, "Wait."

Alex stopped and closed his eyes, barely smothering a groan. "Yeah?"

"We're coming with you."

No. Alex jerked his chin over his shoulder and shook his head. "It's better if y'all stay here. You and Brody could both use the rest."

"I've put Brody down for two naps today, and he's been cooped up in that playpen for the past hour so we could work. He needs some time to play and get some exercise or he won't sleep a wink tonight."

Alex gritted his teeth and tapped the flashlight against his thigh. "Look, it's two miles there and back. That's too much for a child Brody's size, and it'll be dark by the time I head home. It'll be faster if I go by myself. Besides, if you stay here, you can keep an eye out for the horses in case they come wandering back."

"Or," Tammy stressed, eyes flashing, "if we go with you, I can help you look for them while we walk. And when Brody gets tired, I'll carry him." She straightened and took Brody's hand. "I'm sorry. I don't mean to be an aggravation, but it's been two days since I've seen Razz. I can't just sit here and twiddle my thumbs when I could be out looking for her. If I do that, I won't be able to sleep tonight, either."

Her chin trembled and his irritation faded, a sudden surge of sympathy warring with his good sense. It must've shown on his face, because the tension on hers eased and she smiled.

"Please, Alex."

Ah, hell. Just the sweet way his name rolled off her tongue was enough to tip the scales.

"All right," he grumbled. "But stay close and stick to the trail. We're taking a shortcut that goes near the creek, and there are usually snakes."

"Thank you." She held up her pointer finger and rushed to the front porch, then up the steps. "Just let me grab a couple things real quick. You mind watching Brody for a sec?"

Alex sighed. No need to answer. She was gone.

Brody stood silently, staring up at him with a bemused expression. The crooked tilt of the boy's eyebrows was so similar to Dean's. Lord, how that lifted his heavy heart and shot a bolt of pain through him at the same time.

Alex frowned. *He's not Dean. And he's not staying.* He knew he should keep his distance, but his arms yearned to pick the boy up and hug him close.

"So," he said, taking a hesitant step toward Brody

and holding out his hand. "Ready for this walk? It's a mighty long way for a little man like you."

Brody blinked, blew a raspberry, then took off across the grass, babbling. The dog sprang after him, ears and tail flopping. The pair zigzagged across the lawn and into the backyard before Alex managed to round them up.

Fifteen minutes later, they were well on their way up the dirt road. Alex toted the small bag Tammy had packed with diapers and juice, and Tammy guided Brody along the path, keeping him clear of the high grass and deep creek on one side. The sun was strong, hanging low against the horizon, heating their backs and casting a golden glow over the path.

Tammy stopped twice to whistle for her horse, give Brody juice and wipe the baby's rosy cheeks with a damp washcloth.

"If it's too much, we can go back," Alex said. "I can make the trip tomorrow morning."

"No, we're fine." Tammy smiled down at Brody. "Aren't we?"

The baby squealed gibberish, then toddled faster up the road after the frolicking puppy.

"The man we're going to see," Tammy said, stooping to steady Brody as he stumbled over a pothole. "What's his name?"

"Earl Haggert." Alex paused, scanned the path for snakes and wondered how much more he should say. "He goes by Old Earl."

Tammy laughed. "Old Earl? He actually asks people to call him old?"

He shrugged. "His age never seemed to bother him."

Nor did other people's reactions to him.

Alex winced, recalling the first time he and Dean

had encountered Old Earl. They'd been nine years old and heard the rumors circulating around school that Old Earl's property was haunted. That the old man himself was a monster to be feared. And he and Dean had accepted a dare to slip through Earl's fence, spend the night in his hay field and swipe one of his hand-carved wolves from the front porch as proof they'd been there.

Only, Old Earl had caught them sneaking up the front steps, and the sight of his damaged face was so unexpected that they'd screamed their heads off and run.

Alex ducked his head, his face burning. The tales of devils on Earl's land and the darkness of the night might have heightened his and Dean's fright, but being young and stupid was no excuse for their rude, insensitive reaction to the man. Neither he nor Dean had been able to face Earl since then.

As kids, they'd been too afraid. As adults, they'd been too embarrassed.

He'd hate for Tammy to be caught off guard like he and Dean had and risk offending Earl. Old Earl was a good man who just preferred to keep to himself. Something Alex definitely understood and respected.

"Earl is..." He hesitated, searching for the right words. "Well, he's got—"

"Is that the place?"

Tammy pointed at a house on the right. The front yard was littered with tree limbs but immaculate otherwise. Wooden crafts lined the railings of a spotless front porch, and wind chimes tinged together with the gentle breeze, filling the air with a harmonious tune.

"Yeah, that's it," Alex said.

The pup dashed across the front yard and up the

porch steps to scratch at the door. Brody immediately waddled after the dog.

Tammy halted Brody with a gentle hand, lifted him into her arms and whispered over his head, "It's going to be tough to separate these two. You know that, right?"

Alex nodded curtly, his chest aching as Brody squirmed in her arms and reached for the dog.

The door opened, and a deep voice bellowed, "Well, look who finally decided to swagger home."

A bulky figure, clad in denim overalls and a plaid shirt, walked onto the porch and petted the pup. Thick scar tissue wound around his forearms in red and white patches and encased his broad hands.

Alex quickened his step, edging in front of Tammy and Brody as the elderly man approached. "Hey, Earl."

Earl straightened, held out his hand and smiled. "Alex. I haven't seen you in a month of Sundays."

The disfiguring grooves on one side of Earl's face were deep and discolored. Each cluster of burn marks denoted the horrors of the house fire he'd survived years ago. The damaged web of skin marred his jovial expression and produced an uneven tilt to his facial features.

Alex took Earl's hand and lowered his gaze, a prickling sensation spreading through him. It was an odd mixture of respect, admiration and guilt that he always experienced around Earl. Respect and admiration for the other man's bravery and good-hearted, forgiving nature. And guilt from his embarrassing childhood encounter.

"I thought this pup might be yours," Alex said, gesturing toward the Lab as he sat on the wide toe of Earl's boot. "Figured it was time he found his way home."

"Yep, Scout's mine," Earl said. "Don't matter how I

fence him in, he manages to escape. That storm scared off a lot of my dogs, but I've managed to round up most of them. Glad to see you made it through okay." Earl frowned. "Maxine stopped by yesterday and told me about Dean and Gloria." He shook his head, his eyes sad. "Damned shame."

Throat closing, Alex managed a stiff nod and stepped slowly to the side. "Earl, this is Tammy Jenkins and Brod—"

"Brody," Earl interrupted softly, easing down the stairs. His step faltered, however, when a frightened expression crossed the baby's features. "Hey there, fella."

Brody's face crumpled, and he turned, burying his forehead against Tammy's throat and balling his fists into her T-shirt.

Alex cringed and rubbed his hands over his jeans. "Brody just—"

"He's just tired, is all," Tammy chimed. "It was a long walk." She climbed up the two stairs to reach Earl, her bare arm brushing Alex's, and she smiled. "It's nice to meet you. I'm Tammy."

"The barrel racer, eh?" Earl's expression brightened at her nod, and he gestured toward the bandage on her temple. "Maxine told me that twister tore you off the road. Bet you gave it a run for its money, though."

Tammy laughed. "I tried." Her laughter trailed off, and her voice grew heavy. "But some things you can't outrun. I'm just glad I'm still breathing, you know?"

"Yeah," Earl murmured, meeting her eyes and nodding. "I know."

Alex stilled. Something passed between Tammy and Earl. An understanding? Shared emotion? He wasn't sure. But it hung on the air between them, lifting the corners of their mouths into resigned smiles as they exchanged a look.

Then Tammy spoke and the moment was over.

"If it hadn't been for Alex, I probably wouldn't be here." She turned her attention to him, and her smile widened. "He saved my life."

Those beautiful eyes lingered, traveling over his face, then down to his chest and arms, soft and appreciative. Pleasure fluttered through Alex, easing through the numbness under his skin. It'd been so long since a woman had looked at him like that. With approval and subtle—Lord help him—*wanting*.

He grunted and tore his gaze away. She was so young and susceptible. Too young to recognize what a hollow, broken man he was. And too susceptible to an attraction born out of gratitude.

"She's exaggerating," he said, waving a hand in Earl's direction. "I just happened to be in the right place at the right time."

"Watch that, son," Earl chuckled. "If there's one thing I've learned in life, it's to never brush off a compliment from a woman. Those come few and far between for some of us."

Alex ducked his head, feeling like more of a heel than ever. Tammy's sweet compliments, pretty face and bright smile were things he imagined Earl had stopped encountering years ago after he sought seclusion in his isolated home. And Earl deserved them more than he ever would.

Alex sagged with relief when Tammy changed the direction of the conversation.

"I take it you didn't have much damage from the tornado?" Tammy asked.

Earl shook his head. "Nope. Just some broken branches and a roughed-up hay field."

"That's good," she said, eyeing the porch. "Because it'd be a shame to lose all these beautiful crafts. Do you make them yourself?" At Earl's nod, she jiggled Brody gently in her arms and pointed at a wooden dog balanced on the porch rail. "Look, Brody. Do you know what that one is?"

Brody lifted his head and looked at the figurine, darting sideways glances at Earl.

"Need a hint, baby boy?" Earl asked, grinning. "It makes a sound like this…"

Earl barked. Well, howled, really. He did his darnedest to imitate the wooden bloodhound, but his voice cracked and a coughing spell overtook him, doubling him over. A chorus of muffled barks escaped the closed front door, and Scout yipped, then gnawed at his boot.

"Dagnabbit, Scout." Earl shook his leg, laughing and waving his arms in circles as he stumbled. "You bite more than any dog I've come across."

A high-pitched cackle split the air. Brody threw his head back against Tammy's shoulder, his small chest jerking with powerful giggles. Tammy joined him, struggling to keep Brody in her arms as he squirmed and reached for Scout.

Alex smiled, his breath catching at the sheer joy on the baby's face.

"Oh, you like dogs, eh?" Earl spun and opened the front door, and four more puppies streamed out to nip playfully at Scout's ears. "Put that boy on his feet, Tammy, and we'll have some fun."

And it *was* fun. More fun than Alex had experienced in what seemed like forever. The sight of Earl,

Brody and Tammy bumbling around on the front porch, chasing pups and tripping over their own feet, had him chuckling. He sat on the top step and watched, reminiscing over the fun he and Dean used to have as kids.

Alex closed his eyes. How damned wonderful it had felt back then. To be young and have his best friend.

When the trio lost their breaths from exertion and laughter, Earl coaxed Tammy into a rocking chair, set Brody in her lap, then brought out sandwiches and glasses of sweet tea. Alex sipped his drink on the porch steps and tried not to stare at Tammy's graceful movements as she carefully tipped her glass to Brody's lips, wiped the baby's mouth and laughed at Earl's tall tales. They enjoyed each other's company for over an hour and, soon, the golden glow of the setting sun faded and night arrived, bringing with it a full moon that cast a white light over the front porch.

"It's a beautiful night," Earl said, setting his empty cup on the porch rail. "And a long walk home for y'all." He nodded at Alex. "How 'bout a hayride back? I loaded up a few bales on the trailer last week. Just haven't had time to haul 'em off for sale. Bet Brody would like it, and it'd save you another long trek."

Alex glanced at Brody. The baby snuggled deeper into Tammy's embrace, slipped his thumb into his mouth and blinked heavily.

"You want to, Alex?" Tammy asked, studying his face.

Alex tightened his grip on his glass. The gentle plea in her eyes and the exhausted child in her arms made it impossible to refuse the request.

After helping Earl secure the pups inside the house, Alex joined him at the shed while Tammy waited with

Brody on the porch. Alex asked to borrow a chain saw, and after loading it up, he hooked the hay-laden trailer to Earl's truck.

"I think that's good," Earl said, tugging on the chains of the hitch.

Alex nodded and moved away.

"You ever gonna look me in the eye, son?"

Alex stopped. His cheeks warmed beneath Earl's scrutiny. He pressed his palm to the hard metal of the truck and turned his head, forcing himself to meet Earl's gaze.

"You only live a mile down the road, and I rarely see you," Earl said. "You still holding on to the past? 'Cause I don't hold grudges, and I ain't mad at you. Never was."

Alex cringed. "I know."

"No. You don't." Earl sighed and tapped a blunt finger against his damaged face. "When a person has trouble looking, it's usually because they're more uncomfortable with themselves than they are with me. Either that, or they've never encountered a hardship like the one I sport. With you, I suspect it's the former." He frowned. "You and Dean were good boys, Alex. And you've grown into a good man. You got nothing to be ashamed of."

Alex swallowed hard, his tongue clinging to the dry roof of his mouth. "I'm not ashamed."

"Yeah, you are," Earl stressed. "You're ashamed of something." He looked away, peering across the moon-lit lawn toward the front porch. "As for that young gal, she didn't bat an eyelash when she got a good look at me. Not like most people." He nodded. "I think she's seen something a whole lot uglier in her life than that tornado. And she don't seem to be ashamed of nothing."

The corner of his mouth curled up into a small smile. "A man can't help but admire that."

A breeze rustled through the tall grass, and an owl hooted in the trees behind them.

"Night's calling," Earl said. "Better get a move on."

He walked away, climbed into the driver's seat, then revved the engine.

Alex stood still for a moment, absorbing the vibrations of the truck's motor beneath his fingers. "I'm not ashamed," he whispered.

But his voice shook, and the words didn't ring true. His wrist tingled where Tammy had forcefully stilled it two days ago in the hallway of his home, and a bead of sweat trickled down his cheek. He wiped it away with the back of his hand and wondered if Earl was right.

And if so…what kind of ugly had Tammy seen?

SOMETHING ABOUT A clear night sky had always been soothing to Tammy. Maybe it was the shine of the moon or the way the glittering space stretched on endlessly, as though it could swallow up any problem. No matter how big that problem might be.

Tammy tilted her head back for a clearer view of the stars, shifted to a more comfortable position on the hay bale and cradled Brody closer to her chest. Goodness knew she'd encountered her fair share of problems in the past forty-eight hours. A wrecked truck and trailer. She was already a day overdue at Raintree with just a brief message that she was okay having been sent to Jen via the sheriff's office. To save the battery, she kept her cell phone powered off with the exception of an hour in the morning, afternoon and evening, hoping service would return so she could call Jen. It hadn't. Which added to her troubles.

But not finding Razz was, by far, the worst of them.

The thought made her chest burn, the pain fueling her fears of never finding her racing partner. No—her family, really. She'd never been able to trust many people as implicitly as she trusted Razz. Every time she entered the arena with the quarter horse, they were dependent upon each other for success and survival. And she never doubted Razz to deliver either.

"Y'all all right back there?"

Earl's shout barely reached the back of the trailer, but the wave of his broad hand from the truck's window signaled he was checking on them. Just as he had twice since pulling onto the dirt road and heading toward Alex's ranch.

"Yeah," she called back, holding Brody tight with one arm and waving with the other.

The engine rumbled, and the truck moseyed along the path, bumping gently over uneven dirt and crunching over rocks. A tendril of hair blew across her face and caught on her eyelashes for the umpteenth time. She blinked and brushed it back, tucking it behind her ear.

"Too much wind?" Alex eased to the edge of the hay bale facing her and gestured toward the baby in her lap. "There's enough room in the cab for you and Brody if you'd like to sit in there."

"No, thanks. It's a warm night and he's already knocked out." She smiled. "The fresh air will do him good."

The moonlight highlighted Alex's chiseled cheekbones and strong jaw. His gray eyes seemed more mesmerizing than ever beneath the soft glow of the night sky. Tammy dragged her eyes away and looked up again, savoring the pleasure spiraling through her as she recalled the brief kiss from yesterday. Focusing on the tender way his mouth had touched hers was a welcome distraction from her worries about Razz. And her body continued to clamor for more of his attention despite the familiar whisper of caution that always arose when she was around a man.

"I was wondering why you…" Alex cleared his throat. "Well, why you didn't…"

"Hmm?" Tammy prompted, refocusing on Alex. "Why I didn't what?"

He propped his elbows on his thighs and scooted closer, twisting a straw of hay between his knees and asking in a low voice, "Why didn't you ask about Earl's scars?" He frowned and averted his gaze, focusing intently on the hay in his hand. "That's usually the first thing most people ask after meeting him."

"I'm not like most people." She smiled gently as he glanced up. "And I didn't think it'd be polite to ask."

His brow furrowed, and he hesitated, casting a glance at the truck's cab, then asking quietly, "But aren't you curious?"

The soft, sexy rumble of his voice and the moment of shared confidence sent delicious shivers over her skin, and she found herself wanting to coax him into further conversation. "Why?" She leaned in, raised an eyebrow and whispered, "Are you itching to tell me, Mr. Gossip?"

An affronted expression crossed his face. "No." He blinked, shook his head and sat back. "Not at all. I just wondered."

Her mouth twitched. He must've noticed it and the

flirtatious gleam in her eye, because his lean cheeks flushed and he pressed his lips together as though trying to fight a smile. It got the better of him, though, and spread across his face, denting his dimples and casting a boyish look to his face.

"Point taken." He chuckled softly. "I've been duly chastised."

She laughed with him, stopping when he did. He looked away and stared at the dark clusters of trees lining the dirt road. The trailer squeaked over a pothole, and a sad silence filled the space around them.

"Does it really matter how he got them?" she asked, settling Brody more comfortably against her middle. "Earl seems like a nice man. Better than most of the ones I've known."

Alex returned his attention to her, and the intense curiosity in his handsome face made her squirm uneasily on the hay bale.

She straightened and held his gaze. "We all have scars, Alex. It's just that you can't always see them."

Her mouth twisted. She had scars of her own, too. Except she'd been luckier than Earl. There were no visible marks on her body or residual physical pain from the frequent beatings she'd endured beneath her father's fists. But there were still wounds inside. Ones that had formed every time her mother had closed her eyes and walked away, ignoring Tammy's cries for help and choosing her husband over her daughter.

Tammy winced and studied Alex more closely, her eyes drifting over his broad shoulders, chiseled biceps and muscular thighs. He was well built and attractive with no physical flaws she could see. And no one could doubt his loyalty and genuine concern for his friends.

Heck, he'd risked his own safety to help her, and she was nothing more than a stranger to him. But his guarded demeanor hinted that something hid beneath his skin.

What could have driven him to choose to be alone for so long, as Maxine had put it?

"The scars you can't see are usually the worst," Tammy whispered, hugging Brody close and resting her chin on top of his soft hair.

Alex's chest rose on a strong breath, his mouth opening and closing as he met her stare. For a moment, she thought he'd speak, but he didn't. Instead, he nodded, then looked silently at Brody for the remainder of the ride.

A few minutes later, they arrived at Alex's ranch. Earl brought the truck to a stop in the backyard and Alex hopped off the trailer.

"Here," he said, reaching out. "Hold on to Brody and I'll help you down."

Tammy stood, embraced the baby more securely and stepped to the edge of the trailer. His strong hands wrapped around her waist, then eased her down.

Her heart tripped in her chest, making her breath hitch, and she gasped as her boots fumbled over the ground.

"Okay?" Alex asked.

His warm palms lingered on her sides, caressing almost, as he waited for her to get her balance.

"Yes." She tried to ignore the heat and appealing scent of his strong frame as he released her. "Thank you."

The truck door creaked open, and Earl stepped out, his bulky figure outlined in the moonlight. The house cast a shadow over his profile as he approached and the undamaged side of his face became more prominent.

"I expect it's time to tuck that baby in for the night," Earl said, arriving at Tammy's side and rubbing a hand over Brody's back. "As young as he is, though, he'll be raring to go again as soon as the sun comes up."

Tammy laughed and kissed Brody's forehead. He slipped deeper into sleep, his thumb slipping from his open mouth and falling to her chest. "He keeps us on our toes, that's for sure."

"Noticed on the way in that you got your fair share of downed trees." Earl glanced at Alex, then nodded toward the house. "How's your roof?"

Alex sighed. "Needs work. The stable was hit the worst, though."

Tammy's stomach sank, and she scanned the dimly lit land, wishing Razz would somehow miraculously appear.

"I'm available if you need help," Earl said. "How 'bout I swing by in the morning and help you get the tree off your truck? Then we could tackle that roof of yours. My joints have been acting up all day, and that's usually the first sign of rain coming." He smiled. "I could be here at daybreak and, together, I think we could have your truck and roof in good shape by dark."

"Thanks," Alex said, nodding. "I'd appreciate that."

Earl returned to the truck, hopped inside and revved the engine. "I'll be back in the morning with the chain saw. Y'all get that baby a good night's rest, okay?"

"We will," Tammy shouted over the engine.

Brody shifted against her, rubbed his face against her throat, then nuzzled his cheek onto her breast. His small fingers dug deeper into her T-shirt, squeezing rhythmically until a snore escaped and he drifted off again.

Her heart turned over in her chest. She kissed his forehead and cradled him closer. The weight of him in her arms filled some of the emptiness inside her, and she stood still under the full moon and bright stars, absorbing the peace.

"Both of you need a good night's rest."

Tammy started at the gruff sound of Alex's voice. He reached out slowly and covered her hand with his on Brody's back. Her skin danced beneath the warm weight of his broad thumb as it swept gently across her wrist.

"Follow me?" he asked softly.

The tender light in his eyes and gentle smile made every inch of her eager to follow. She pulled in a deep breath and nodded.

He led the way into the house, guiding her carefully up the front porch steps with a flashlight he pulled from his pocket, then drew to a halt in the kitchen.

"Wait here a minute, okay?"

She did, watching as he disappeared around the corner and listening in the dark kitchen as he rustled around in another room. Light pooled onto the kitchen floor again as he reappeared, motioning with the flashlight toward the hall.

"First door on the left," he said, his fingers rubbing over something in his palm.

She proceeded down the hall, then stopped in front of the door. Her hand lifted toward the doorknob but froze in midair. "I thought you never used this room."

The familiar heat of him drew close to her back, and his soft breath tickled her neck. He eased a brawny arm around her and slid a key into the lock. "I don't," he whispered. "But I'll make an exception for Brody."

The lock clicked, and he shoved the door open. He swept the flashlight over the interior of the room, highlighting baby blue walls, a wooden chest, a rocking chair, a changing table and…a crib. Every item was pristine and arranged in a welcoming semicircle.

She swung her head to the side, stilling as her lips brushed the rough stubble of his jaw. Heart pounding, she fought the desire to nuzzle her cheek against his skin and asked, "Why do you have—"

"Nothing was damaged in here," he said, voice husky. "The crib sheets are in the chest, and once you get Brody settled, you can have my room to yourself for the night."

"But, Alex—"

"Not tonight, okay?" He lowered his head, his mouth moving against her temple and his broad palm settling on her hip. "Let's just get some rest. We all need it."

Of its own accord, her body sank back against his. She fit perfectly, his wide chest and muscular thighs cradling her as though she belonged there. A peaceful tenderness welled inside her, quieting that inner voice of caution and strengthening so much it filled her eyes, blurring her vision.

Alex pressed the flashlight into her palm at Brody's back, his fingers trembling. "Good night."

He left, and moments later, a cabinet thudded, then glass clinked. She imagined him standing at the kitchen sink, taking shots as he had the first night she'd arrived, and wondered why a man who kept such a careful distance from children would've invested so much in the future of having one.

Her throat tightened as another thought hit her. Had he lost a child? Was that why he was no longer married?

Tammy clung tighter to Brody, wanting, more than anything, to wrap her arms around Alex and hold him just as close.

Chapter Five

"There are a few things in life a woman just needs."

Tammy stopped sweeping the front porch, propped her hand on her hip and leveled what she hoped was a stern expression on Brody. But it was difficult to keep her frown in place when he looked up at her from the top step and grinned. His tiny feet inched their way down to the next step despite her ten thousand requests to stay put. The same requests he'd ignored throughout the morning as she'd cleaned the house while Alex and Earl worked on the roof.

Clearly, the comfortable slumber in the crib last night had replenished his energy.

"Say, for instance," Tammy continued, "I'd kill for a hot shower right now." She dragged her fingers through her dingy hair, the tangled, straw-like strands making her cringe. "And a huge bottle of conditioner."

Three days without power or running water didn't make for the best beauty regimen. She dipped her head, eyed her rumpled T-shirt, then frowned. Of course, the fact that the tornado had flung her overnight bags from her truck, leaving them pinned beneath the overturned trailer in the mud, hadn't helped matters, either. She'd spent over an hour sifting through soaked shirts and underwear for a decent outfit after the wrecker hauled away her truck.

Brody smiled wider, gripped the edge of the bricks with both hands and shimmied down to the next step.

"A cheeseburger would be great, too." Her mouth twitched as he stretched the toes of his sneakers toward the next one. "One piled with bacon and a big side of onion rings. You know, the whole shebang. Unfortunately, there's no chance of that."

Brody slipped to the lowest step and glanced up at her, his shoes only inches from the grass.

"But what I need most of all," Tammy said, propping the broom against the porch rail, "is for a certain little boy to listen to me when I tell him no."

Brody turned his head, pointed at the front lawn and squealed as a golden ball of fur darted across the grass.

"I know you want to play with Scout."

Good grief, did she know. When Earl arrived at first light, Scout had shown up shortly after, having followed Earl's truck to the ranch, and had remained underfoot ever since. Apparently, Brody's love for the puppy was reciprocated.

"But," Tammy added, "I can't finish sweeping this porch and chase after you and Scout at the same time, now can I?"

Brody grinned mischievously and scooted to the edge of the step.

"Don't do it." Tammy took a slow step forward, smiling as he stood. "Don't. You. Do it…"

Brody cackled and took off, his jeans and diaper swishing with every step.

Tammy darted down the steps and chased him around Alex's truck, which Earl and Alex had freed from the fallen tree. Scout joined Brody in the chase, and Tammy continued to play along, stumbling over the dog and laughing.

"That's it, Brody," Earl called out from the roof. "Give her a run for her money."

Tammy caught Brody, hugged him to her middle and looked up. Alex and Earl stood on the roof, shading their eyes from the sun and chuckling down at them. Alex's T-shirt, soaked with sweat, clung to his muscular frame and sent a wave of wanting over her.

"Don't encourage him, Earl," Tammy said, forcing her attention from Alex to the other man. "I've already had to—"

A strong buzzing started in Tammy's back pocket. She froze in place, then scrambled to pull her cell phone free of her sweaty jeans. The red battery at the top of the display indicated the charge was almost depleted, but was it finally receiving calls? The lit screen displaying "Jen" in the center proved it was. Hallelujah!

"It's working," Tammy shouted. She kissed Brody's cheek, then jumped up and down, waving the phone in the air. "We have cell service! That means the power may be back on soon."

Alex and Earl exchanged an amused glance, then made their way to the ladder and started climbing down. Tammy swiped the screen and squealed hello into the receiver.

"Oh, thank heavens. I've been worried sick about you." Jen's voice held equal amounts of frustration and concern. "Every time I've called, your phone has been off, and you haven't answered any of my text messages."

"I couldn't," Tammy said, a relieved laugh bursting past her lips. "Cell service has been out and the landlines were down. There was no power because of the tornado—"

Jen gasped. "Are you all right? The sheriff sent word that you were okay, but I needed to hear your voice."

"I'm fine. But my truck took a beating."

"The storms have been all over the news the past couple of days. Colt said he didn't think you normally took that route, but after the sheriff called, he went out of his mind worrying about you."

Tammy winced. Colt Mead, Jen's fiancé and Tammy's cousin, had answered Tammy's call for help years ago when her father's beatings had become too severe to endure. Colt had picked her up the same day, and they'd eventually ended up on the rodeo circuit, where Colt began bull riding. After they met Jen, the three of them had toured the circuit together for years until Colt's father was killed in a tragic accident. Colt left the circuit to take care of his younger sister and asked Jen to help him temporarily. But *temporary* turned into permanent after Colt and Jen fell in love, then decided to retire and settle down at Raintree Ranch to raise Colt's sister.

"Please tell Colt I'm fine," Tammy said, grabbing unsuccessfully at Brody's waistband as he toddled away. "I'm stuck here for the moment, since my truck isn't drivable, but I made it through okay."

"Where are you? We'll come get you." There were scuffling sounds on the other end of the line. "Just tell me the address and we'll leave right away."

"No, please wait. My battery is about to die and I don't have long, so please listen for a sec, okay?" Tammy gripped the phone tighter and hustled across the lawn, chasing Brody. "How are plans for the wedding coming? Is everything working out?"

"Everything's going well," Jen said. "I've got more than enough help and my mom is in wedding planner heaven." Her laugh was brief. "It's just that Colt and I miss you."

"I miss you, too. But would you mind if I stayed and helped someone out for a couple of weeks, then came to Raintree a bit later? I promise I'll be there in time for the rehearsal dinner. There's no way I'd miss it." She caught up with Brody, wrapped an arm around his waist and halted him before he reached a pile of debris by the driveway. "It's just that someone helped me out and I kind of owe him a favor."

Brody whined and strained in her hold, wiggling against her chest and jostling the phone.

"What was that?" Jen asked.

"The favor." Tammy released Brody, allowing him to run across a safer part of the grass, then followed him to the other side of the lawn. "The storm was bad, Jen. It did a lot of damage. Razz is missing, and it left a little boy orphaned. It would've done me in, too, if it hadn't been for Alex."

"Alex?"

"That's who I'm staying with while my truck is fixed. And until I find Razz. I can't leave until I know what happened to her." She cleared her throat to erase the shakiness from her voice. "Besides, Alex saved my life, and the least I can do is help him out."

Tammy watched as Brody plopped onto the grass with Scout and quickly filled Jen in on what had happened, cringing each time the low-battery signal dinged across the line.

"So it's just the three of you staying out there?" Jen

asked. "Are you sure this Alex is trustworthy? I mean, you just met him."

"I know. But he's different."

Tammy dragged her teeth over her bottom lip and sneaked a glance at Alex. He walked up the front steps, flipped the porch light switch on, then eyed the fixture. When it didn't illuminate, he looked in her direction and shook his head, smiling sadly.

Tammy turned away, face heating, and lowered her voice. "*I'm* different with him. And after what we went through…" She pulled in a deep breath, searching for the right words. "I don't know how to explain it, but I think I'm safe with him."

"Sounds like he's made quite an impression."

"He has." Tammy smiled, her belly fluttering as she recalled his gentle kiss and touches. "He's a good man, and I owe him." She pressed the phone tighter to her ear, waiting for Jen to speak. When she didn't, Tammy asked, "What is it? You're never this quiet."

"I'm just thinking."

"About what?" Tammy pressed. "You can always be honest with me."

Jen remained silent for a moment, then said, "I know how difficult it is to be on the road alone, and I'm sorry Colt and I left like we did. We're still family, and there's always a place for you at Raintree if you get tired of the circuit." She sighed. "This is really none of my business, but I love you like a sister and you've been through so much. Please don't take this the wrong way, Tammy, but could how you met Alex have affected the way you see him?"

Her stomach tensed. She focused on the jagged line

of trees on the other side of the grounds. "No. He *is* different. He's a good man."

"I'm not saying he isn't," Jen said hastily. "And I'm glad he helped you. But that doesn't obligate you to him in any way. Of course, I'll support you in whatever you choose to do. I just worry about you staying in the middle of nowhere with a stranger. And I worry about you getting too attached too fast and getting hurt. Could you please just think about it? For me? Just ask yourself if you think about this man the way you do because Colt and I are no longer with you. And, well, without Razz…" She hesitated. "Is it because you feel alone?"

Tammy closed her eyes, cheeks burning and throat thickening. "I—" Her voice broke. She opened her eyes and tried again. "I don't…"

Two thick figures moved between the broken trees across the field.

Tammy squinted against the sharp rays of the sun, stilling as identifiable shapes emerged from between the stripped branches. Two muzzles appeared, then broad necks, long legs and tails.

"I'm sorry, I've got to go," Tammy whispered, cutting the call and shoving the phone in her pocket.

She watched silently as the two horses cleared the tree line and ambled into the center of the field. They stopped and stood motionless, side by side. The distance and glare of the sun made it impossible to decipher the color of their hides.

"Razz?" Tammy lifted a shaky hand to her mouth and whistled around her fingers.

The horses didn't respond. She took a jerky step forward.

"Easy." Alex's broad palm touched the small of her

back, his voice soft. "We don't know which horses they are or what state they're in. Let me check them first."

"I'm going with you," she said.

Alex frowned. "Tammy—"

"Let her go," Earl said. "She knows what she's up against. If one of the horses is hers, she has the right to do what needs to be done if necessary."

Tammy flinched, her stomach churning. She didn't know what she'd do if she found Razz mortally wounded. But she couldn't stand the thought of never knowing what happened to her.

Earl walked to Brody's side and petted Scout. "Y'all go ahead. Brody and I will wait here."

Brody smiled up at Earl, babbling and pointing at Scout's rapidly wagging tail. Tammy's eyes lingered on Brody, and she drew strength from the boy's bright expression before meeting Alex's solemn gaze.

"Ready?" he asked.

Tammy nodded, and they walked slowly across the field. As they approached, Tammy scrutinized the horses' mud-slicked hides for Razz's black-and-white pattern. The thick sludge coating the majority of their bodies made it difficult, but she managed to discern a broad black-and-white marking on one horse's chest.

"Razz?"

Eyes swollen, both horses remained motionless with their ears meekly back and tails still. Though she didn't respond, the horse on the left was definitely Razz.

Tammy stepped forward. "Hey, girl."

Razz flinched and stepped back. The horse on the right followed suit, pressing close to Razz's side. The sun dipped lower at their backs, and the wet streaks of tears on the mare's cheeks glistened. Bright patches of blood mixed with the mud on both horses' hides, denoting gashes and punctures on their shoulders, hips and legs.

Tammy held her breath, stifling a sob, and clenched her fists at her sides. She didn't know what was worse—the days spent not knowing where Razz was at all, or finding Razz so badly wounded that she'd be forced to put her down.

"She's been hurt so much," she whispered, throat tightening.

Alex's warm palm enveloped hers and squeezed. "We don't know anything for sure yet." He waited until she looked up, his gray eyes kind and reassuring. "Let me take a look at her, all right?"

Unable to speak, she nodded. Alex released her hand and moved slowly toward Razz. He spoke softly, his voice low and gentle. Tammy couldn't make out the words, but the tone was enough to help her catch her breath and unfurl her fists.

It seemed to have the same effect on Razz. She stood still as Alex approached and continued to stand motionless as he cupped her cheek gently, allowing him to stroke her jaw.

Alex continued to murmur in a soft tone and Razz responded, lowering her muzzle and nudging Alex's forehead with her own. Alex praised her, then began checking her injuries, moving slowly from her head to tail and carefully examining her wounds. He repeated the process with the second horse and returned to stroke Razz's neck.

"The other horse is mine," Alex said. "Razz and Sapphire are hurt pretty badly." He smiled. "But they're gonna be okay."

"How do you know for sure?" Her voice pitched

higher, tremors coursing through her limbs. "What if there's more damage than you think?"

His smile slipped, and his handsome features gentled. "If that's the case, we'll cross that bridge when we get to it. But from what I can tell, their wounds will heal."

Hot tears scalded her cheeks, and she blinked rapidly, eyes darting over Razz's wounds. "Are you sure?"

"Tammy, look at me." Alex moved into her line of vision, his deep voice calm but firm. "Razz is going to be okay." He reached out and cradled her jaw with his palm, his thumb wiping a tear from her cheek. "We'll make sure of it."

Tammy's shoulders sagged with relief, and she managed a shaky smile.

"Help me lead them to the stable?" Alex asked, stepping back.

Tammy wiped her face with the back of her hand and cleared her throat. "Of course." She eased past Alex and crossed to Razz's side. "Hi, girl," she whispered, touching the mare's shoulder.

Razz dipped her head and took a step closer.

"I told you I wouldn't leave you." Tammy slipped her arms around Razz and pressed her cheek against the horse's neck.

She breathed in the familiar scent of her racing partner, her chest swelling with joy and a fresh round of tears trickling down her face to mingle with Razz's. After a few moments, Razz made a soft sound of pleasure, and Sapphire moved close for soothing pats, too.

Tammy laughed and glanced at Alex. "You're right. I think they're going to be okay."

Alex smiled, his charming dimples appearing, and nodded.

That flutter in her belly returned, unfurling and spreading through her in a rush of pleasure. There he stood. Broad and muscular. Gentle and protective. A tower of tender strength in another seemingly hopeless situation, providing things she hadn't known she needed. Understanding and reassurance. Support. And every inch of her body wanted to press against his, wrap around him and hold on tight.

Is it because you feel alone?

Tammy stilled, Jen's words flitting through her mind. She studied Alex, her eyes traveling over his handsome face, the warmth of his expression and his solid presence.

Maybe. Maybe she did feel alone. But at least she *did* feel when she was with Alex. She felt more alive than she had in her entire life. She wanted Alex so much that the dance of desire beneath her skin overrode her fears and insecurities. And singing Brody to sleep in the nursery last night had made her dream of a home and children of her own almost...*tangible.*

She wasn't ready to let those feelings go. Not yet.

Tammy released Razz, walked over to Alex and wrapped her arms around him. She hugged him close, pressing her body to his and savoring the strong throb of his heart against her breasts. "Thank you."

ALEX APPLIED ONE last strip of tape to the gauze on Sapphire's leg wound, then sat back on his haunches in the stall. "There, gorgeous. Now you can rest."

Sapphire looked down at him and released a soft breath, her swollen eyelids blinking heavily.

Alex grimaced, then reached up and stroked her leg. After he and Tammy had settled the horses into the two least damaged stalls, Earl had driven ten miles to contact the nearest vet. It'd taken almost the entire afternoon for the vet to tend to Razz's and Sapphire's most severe injuries, and Alex and Tammy had taken over the more minor ones after he'd left.

It'd been an exhausting process for all of them. Most especially Brody, whom Earl had taken inside two hours ago to keep entertained. But it was worth it to know Razz and Sapphire would heal and could finally rest easy for the night.

"I've never seen such a perfect blue roan." Tammy entered the stall, then knelt at his side, her green eyes roving over Sapphire.

Alex couldn't stop the proud smile spreading across his face. A thorough washing had highlighted the blue sheen of Sapphire's hide and powerful build. And though he was a long way from recouping his losses, Sapphire's return kindled a spark of hope within him that, perhaps, more horses had survived.

Tammy curled her slim fingers around his knee and smiled up at him. "Sapphire is beautiful."

He studied her, absorbing the pink flush in her cheeks, the tempting curve of her soft lips and the trusting adoration in her gaze.

Hell, *she* was beautiful.

The press of her soft curves as she'd hugged him hours earlier had eased through the thin cotton of his T-shirt and still lingered on his skin. Her embrace had heated his blood and stirred long-buried desires to life, making him feel as though he was important to someone. A part of something. As though he belonged.

Damned if those yearnings hadn't begun to hinder his good sense. And their talk of scars yesterday had tempted him to imagine she might be different. That maybe she looked for what a person had rather than what a person lacked.

Even so, it was a bad idea to get tangled up with a woman who was leaving soon, and it'd be even worse to take advantage of her hero worship.

His stomach dropped. That was all it was. Hero worship. The kind he hoped would stay solid until she left, obscuring his flaws and hiding them from her forever. Then, at least, he'd remain a man in Tammy's eyes.

His mouth twisted. Unlike with Susan.

Alex pressed his palms flat against the floor, the shavings poking between the gaps in his fingers as he fought against gripping Tammy's hip, tugging her tight to his side and covering her mouth with his own.

"She's got a strong heart," he said, tearing his eyes from Tammy and glancing up at Sapphire. "Sapphire and Razz were in better shape than I thought they'd be after being gone for so many days. Sapphire knows the land. She must've led Razz to the creek for water, then found her way home and brought Razz with her."

"I'm glad she did."

Tammy leaned in closer, her soft breath tickling his ear and her small hand warming his skin through the thick denim of his jeans.

Heart skipping, he shoved to his feet and glanced in the neighboring stall. "Razz settling down okay?"

"Yeah." Tammy stood, too, then shoved her hands in her back pockets. The action pulled her T-shirt tight against the full curves of her breasts. "She's already drifting off."

Alex averted his eyes. "A full belly, good doctoring and a comfortable place to rest…" He shrugged to relieve the tension in his shoulders. "They'll probably sleep for a day or two straight."

Tammy laughed. "I'm kind of wanting that, too." She dragged a hand through her dark hair, wincing as her fingers tangled in the wavy strands. "I'd give anything to soak in a bubble bath, then wallow around on a soft bed in an air-conditioned room."

His eyes shot straight to her long legs, curvy hips and ample breasts, the idea of her sprawled on a bed, soft and welcoming, fanning that spark of desire into flame.

She held up a hand and smiled. "Not that your bed isn't comfortable. As a matter of fact, I've enjoyed sleeping on it."

Ah, hell. His bed. A fresh set of images flashed through his mind. Ones that made his body tighten uncomfortably. Alex dragged a hand across the back of his neck and cleared his throat, heat searing his face.

She laughed, the full-bodied sound echoing around the stall. "Did I embarrass you?" Her expression was full of surprise. And, oddly enough, delight. "Because embarrassing you wasn't what I was going for." Seemingly emboldened, she stepped closer and placed a hand on his chest. "Though it's nice to know I affect you in at least one way."

Her gentle teasing made his heart trip, the tender flirtation prompting him to recall what his life had been like years ago. When he didn't balk at stripping himself bare, holding a woman close and letting her in. When he enjoyed exploring the depths of her heart, searching for her secrets and sharing his. Back when he believed himself to be solid. And whole.

"One way?" Before he knew it, his hand drifted around her back to settle between her shoulder blades, and his head lowered, his mouth moving against the soft skin of her temple as he whispered, "You have no idea how many ways."

She pulled in a swift breath, her green eyes darkening as she slid her hand up and wove her fingers through his hair. Her touch was confident, but she trembled against him as though unsure.

He froze, her potential uncertainty yanking him back to reality. He was a far cry from the man she thought he was. And he was experienced enough to recognize the dangers of her youthful naïveté and hesitation. If they took this any further, they'd both walk away empty. This was *not* a good idea.

"Tammy." He released her hip, tugged her hand from his neck and stepped back. "This isn't—"

"Alex?"

Earl's faint call came on the heels of the creak of the stable door.

Grateful for the interruption, Alex slipped out of the stall, trying to ignore the wounded look in Tammy's eyes and fighting the urge to return and scoop her into his arms.

Brody ran down the center aisle of the stable with Scout nipping at the laces of his sneakers.

Earl followed at a much slower pace, then stopped, sighing deeply. "Y'all finished doctoring those horses?" At Alex's nod, Earl tugged a rag from his pocket and dabbed at his forehead. "Good." He gestured toward Brody. "I've been trying to entertain that rascal for a while now, and I've run out of things to keep him occupied."

The baby cackled, then dropped to all fours, attempting to crawl between Alex's legs.

"Hold up, buddy." Alex bent and lifted Brody to his

feet. "You can't crawl around on this floor. There's still too much junk lying around."

Brody wiggled against his hands and scowled up at him. Something green speckled his cheeks and forehead. It also clung to his hair and caked the front of his overalls. Scout bounced at Brody's side, licking at the stains with each jump.

"Why is he green?" Tammy knelt beside Brody, nudged Scout away and wiped Brody's cheeks with the hem of her T-shirt.

"Oh, that'd be the peas," Earl said. "He got hungry and I tried to feed him some of that jarred baby food I found in the kitchen. But that didn't work out too well." He wrinkled his nose. "Neither did the diaper changing."

Brody released a frustrated squeal, batting at Tammy's hands as she scrubbed at his food-splattered face.

"I think he just got to missing y'all." Earl walked over, kissed Brody's head, then headed for the door. "I gotta get home and let the rest of the dogs out while there's still an hour of daylight left." He paused, glanced around the stable, then looked at Alex. "Need some more help tomorrow? I could help you spruce up a bit in here."

Alex smiled. It'd been so long since he'd had company besides Dean and Gloria. Earl had been a huge help in more ways than one, and he'd enjoyed the other man's wild tales and crass jokes throughout the earlier part of the day. He was already looking forward to working with him again. Not to mention he could definitely use the help—though he couldn't afford to pay very much.

"I'd like that," Alex said. "But you've got to let me pay you."

Earl held up a hand. "No need for that. We're friends."

"I know, but—"

"I tell you what." Earl pointed at Scout. "You take that pup off my hands for a while, and that'd be payment enough. It'd be nice not to have my feet chomped on for a few days, and I think Brody would enjoy having him around."

Alex laughed. "Sounds good."

Earl waved goodbye to Tammy, then left, whistling.

"Oh, what a sweet mess." Tammy giggled as Brody forced his way past her attempts to clean his face and hugged her neck. His legs lifted restlessly as he attempted to climb into her arms. "That creek you've been talking about…" Tammy stood, lifting Brody and settling him on her hip. "Is it deep enough to wade in?"

"Yeah." Alex smiled as Scout started gnawing the hem of Tammy's jeans.

"Deep enough to bathe in?" Tammy frowned and shook her leg as Scout growled.

Alex nodded.

"Good. I think it's time we all cleaned up, and since there's still no power, we'll just have to hunt running water down at the creek." She grinned and started for the door. Scout slid along with her, his teeth latched on to her jeans. "I'll grab my conditioner, then you can lead the way."

An ache bloomed in his lower belly. A creek and bathing meant a wet, tempting Tammy.

He spun away and shut the door on Sapphire's stall, taking longer than usual to secure the latch. "I'll take you down there, then leave you to it."

Her footsteps halted. "I'm going to need your help, Alex. Brody is a mess, and I can't wash my hair and hold on to him at the same time. And trust me, another bird bath in the sink with bottled water isn't going to get the job done."

Alex glanced over his shoulder. "Then I'll bathe Brody here and put him to bed while you clean up. Give you some peace and quiet for a while."

Tammy shook her head. "I think Brody would prefer us all to go together."

And spend the last hour of daylight fighting to keep his hands off her? *Hell, no.* He planned to go inside, extinguish his lust with a shot of whiskey, then crash on the couch. Alone.

"Brody's too young to care either way. I'm staying here."

Her eyes narrowed, and she squared her shoulders.

Ten minutes later, Alex stood, arms crossed, with his back to the creek and scowled at the feminine pair of jeans draped over a bush. The shiny stitching on the back pockets seemed to wink at him as the sun dropped close to the horizon, forcing him to recall just how well Tammy's curves filled out the denim.

"Okay," Tammy called over the rush of the creek. "Brody is fresh and clean again."

Water splashed, then twigs snapped. Scout scuttled by, stopped to shake his wet fur, then stretched out on the grass.

"Would you take Brody, please, so I can wash my hair?"

Alex tensed, the soft, melodic sound of her voice sending excited shivers up the back of his neck. Lord, how he wanted her lying next to him on a bed, her teasing words whispering across white cotton sheets and tickling his ear—

Brody shouted, the sharp sound causing Alex to jump.

"He wants to go back into the water," Tammy said. "Do you mind?"

Alex grunted, then reached up with both hands, tugged his shirt over his head and tossed it on a pile of towels on the ground. Turning, he closed his eyes and thrust his arms out.

Tammy laughed. "I appreciate the fact that you're a gentleman, Alex, but I'm wearing a bra and underwear, which covers more than most swimsuits nowadays." Her wet fingertips tapped his forearm. "You're going to have to open your eyes to hold on to Brody properly."

Reluctantly, he did. He tried his damnedest to keep his attention above her collarbones, but his eyes strayed anyway, snagging on the thin material of her bra. It was the same shade of green as her eyes and plastered to her breasts, leaving little to the imagination.

God, help me.

"You…uh…" Tammy's voice faltered, squeaking slightly. Brody squirmed against her. "Are you going to wear your boots in the water?"

Alex refocused on her face. Her eyes left his boots, lingered over his jeans-clad hips, then lifted to his bare chest. A blush snaked down her neck, and her mouth parted enticingly, bringing a smile to his face.

"Nope." His mouth quirked, and he had a sudden urge to test how far her bravado would stretch. "Not gonna wear my jeans, either."

He pulled off his boots and socks, unbuttoned his jeans, then reached for the zipper.

She watched until it rasped halfway down, then her eyes darted skyward, looking everywhere but at him. "Just let me know when you're ready for Brody."

He laughed, finished removing his jeans, then reached for the baby. "Here, I'll take him."

She held Brody out, her eyes still avoiding him.

"I appreciate you trying to protect my virtue and all," he teased, "but I'm wearing boxers."

Tammy laughed, then met his eyes as she handed Brody over. "Your virtue's safe with me. For the moment."

Alex raised an eyebrow at her mischievous expression, then waded into the creek with Brody. He spent the next few minutes distracting himself from Tammy's graceful movements as she bathed by holding Brody at a safe height in the water while the baby kicked and babbled.

Alex smiled. "So you like water, huh?"

Brody squealed and slapped the surface. A spray of water hit Alex in the face, stinging his eyes. He grimaced. Brody cackled and bounced harder in Alex's arms, the sheer joy in his face so reminiscent of Dean's fun-loving nature.

"Your daddy liked the water, too." Alex smiled, an ache returning to his chest. "We used to go swimming out here every summer." He swallowed hard, his throat burning. "Those days were the best ones of my life."

Brody stared up at him, his gaze drifting from Alex's forehead down to his chin, then he reached up and tugged at Alex's hair.

Alex laughed and drew Brody closer. "Yeah. We were a lot younger then, and I didn't have all this gray."

He gently untangled Brody's fingers from his hair,

then examined the baby's hand as it nestled within his own. Brody's palm was so small against his, but the tiny fingers curled tight around his thumb and squeezed, proving there was more strength in that little body than he might've initially guessed. The firm tug traveled up his forearm, across his shoulder, then seeped into his chest, blurring his vision.

"I know you miss your daddy as much as your mama. Your daddy was a good man," Alex whispered. "One of the best."

He didn't know how long he stayed still in the water, studying the color of Brody's eyes, the shape of his nose and the playful expressions that flitted across the baby's face. All he knew as Brody's small chest lifted against his rhythmically was that Brody was breathing. He was strong and alive. And every beat of that baby's heart meant that, in some small way, Dean would go on living, too.

"Alex?"

He blinked and dragged his eyes from Brody. Tammy sat at the edge of the creek with a towel wrapped around her, watching him with a concerned expression as the last bit of daylight began to fade.

"Are you okay?" she asked softly.

"Yeah." He stilled at the husky note in his voice, realizing the wetness coating his cheeks was no longer creek water. He scrubbed a hand over his face. "I'm fine."

Brody resumed splashing and babbling.

"I think the power's back on," Tammy said, gesturing toward the field behind her. "I can see a light over in the direction of the house. I think it's the porch light you turned on earlier." She hesitated. "Are you ready to go in?"

Alex looked down at Brody, peace settling sweetly inside him as the baby laughed and splashed in the water. Then he looked at Tammy, savoring the gentle tone in her voice and the patient tenderness in her eyes.

He smiled. "Not yet. Would you mind if we stayed a little longer?"

"Not at all." She returned his smile, hugged her knees to her chest, then whispered, "I'd like that a lot."

Chapter Six

A sweet satisfaction existed in hard work. The kind Alex never failed to appreciate.

"Feels good, don't it?"

Alex lowered his glass of iced tea, stretched his legs out across the porch steps, then smiled up at Earl. "Sure does."

Earl laughed, then tipped his glass up and drank heavily, the clink of ice mingling with his contented groan.

One perk of the power coming back on was being able to enjoy a cold drink in the late-afternoon sun. And after a week and a half of repairing the stable, caring for the horses and clearing fallen trees from the field, Alex had every intention of soaking it up.

Apparently, Scout did, too. He ran from one end of the newly cleared field to the other, stopping to snuffle and roll around in the grass every few feet.

Alex chuckled, propped his elbows on the top step behind him and closed his eyes. His T-shirt clung to his sweat-slicked back and his jeans had become stiflingly hot, but, hell, what did that matter after all he'd accomplished over the past few days? The steady progress in reparations to the ranch had returned a sense of control to the day. And each newly restored section of the stable and fields, however small, made him think he actually had a say in what the future held for him.

Which was the exact opposite of how he'd felt after attending Dean and Gloria's funeral last week. That had been one of the longest days of his life and he'd been anxious to get back to the ranch with Tammy to resume a sense of normalcy. And help Brody find the same.

A squeal pierced his eardrums, then a small body climbed over his shoulder and onto his chest, almost dislodging the glass from his hand.

"Brody, wait."

Alex caught the baby with one arm and held his iced tea up with the other as Tammy ran up behind him. "Aw, he's all right." He sat up, cradling Brody to his midsection and tipped his drink toward him. "You want some of this, too, little man?"

Brody babbled, reached out and tugged the glass toward his mouth.

The sun glinted off the glass, and Alex squinted up at Tammy. "Is it okay for him to have some?"

"I put a lot of sugar in it, so it's not good for his teeth." Tammy grinned. "But I don't think a little will hurt."

Alex smiled, admiring the pretty blush in her cheeks and playful sparkle in her eyes, but he wasn't sure he agreed with her comment. He'd spent only a little time at the creek with her and Brody last week, but that brief hour had been enough to keep the image of her tempting mouth and soft curves reemerging behind his eyelids each night despite his attempts to sleep in the recently restored guest room.

She'd managed to slip farther past his guard than he'd realized, and the thought should've prompted him to keep his distance. Instead, he found himself wanting to spend more time with her. Wanting to enjoy more of her feisty banter, warm laugh and gentle flirtations.

Brody fussed, and Alex glanced down, tipping the glass carefully to the baby's lips and helping him sip the tea. Brody grinned, licked his lips and reached for more.

Tammy laughed, bringing Alex's eyes back to her. He wasn't sure if the way she'd helped him heal with Brody last week was the cause of the lingering gratitude he had for her or not. But he wanted to keep her as smiling and content as she was now, without a trace of the fear or panic that had shadowed her expression when she'd first arrived.

"Looks like Ms. Maxine is making the rounds again today." Earl nodded toward the driveway, where a small car eased up the path, dust particles dancing in the sun behind it.

Alex set his glass down, stood with Brody in his arms, then walked over to greet Maxine.

"Now, isn't this a sight?" Maxine chimed as she exited the car and shut the door. "I guess you figured out how to handle a baby after all, hmm?"

Alex smiled. Maxine beamed up at him, then leaned in and kissed Brody's cheek. Brody patted her cheek, then pointed toward Scout in the field.

"We were just having iced tea," Tammy said, walking up with Earl. "Would you like a glass?"

"Oh, no, thank you, Tammy. I can only stay a minute. I've got business to tend to but thought I'd stop by and give you this." She held out something square, which was wrapped in a white cloth. "Sam at the auto body shop found it this morning when he was working on your truck. He thought you'd like to keep it safe while your repairs are being finished."

Tammy took it and removed the cloth, revealing a cracked glass case with a gold buckle mounted inside. World Champion was etched across the top edge of the glass in elegant script.

Alex stilled, securing his grip on Brody as the baby leaned over and grabbed at it. "You won at Vegas last year?"

Tammy smiled, her fingers drifting slowly over the large words. "*We* won at Vegas." She nodded toward the stable. "I told you Razz was fast."

"Well, what do you know?" Earl poked his head over Tammy's shoulder for a better look at the medal, then winked at Alex. "You had a celebrity in the house all this time and didn't even know it."

An uneasiness settled in Alex's gut. *World champion. Celebrity.* They were stark reminders of the differences in his and Tammy's lifestyles. And an even more unwelcome reminder of how little they knew about each other.

He forced a tight smile and tried to shrug off the awkward tension knotting between his shoulder blades. Had the traumatic experiences of the past weeks clouded his judgment more than he'd thought? Was the newfound connection he'd begun to feel with Tammy no more than misplaced grief?

Hell, he should've been more worried about himself falling prey to a compulsive attraction rather than Tammy.

"...update."

Alex refocused on Maxine. "I'm sorry, what did you say?"

"I said, I also stopped by to give you an update on

Brody's situation." Maxine reached out and brushed a wisp of hair from Brody's forehead. "I finally got in touch with Dean's half brother, John Nichols, and explained the situation." She frowned. "I didn't realize how little he and Dean had to do with each other, and I'm not sure he'll come forward. John just turned twenty-one and got engaged. He and his fiancée agreed to think it over and will let me know in a week or two if they're willing to take responsibility for Brody. If he doesn't let me know by then, I'll need to take Brody to the children's home in Atlanta."

Alex stiffened, his arms tightening around Brody. What a fool he was. He'd known this was only temporary, so this wasn't a surprise. But it didn't dull the pain throbbing in his chest at the thought of Brody leaving. Or quell the panic that arose at the thought of losing the last connection he had to Dean.

"But Brody will stay here for now, right?" Tammy curved her hand around Alex's biceps, staring at Maxine as though pleading for confirmation. "With us?"

Maxine remained silent as she scrutinized Tammy's face, then glanced at Alex. "Yes," she said, a small smile appearing. "Brody will stay with you for now."

Tammy's relieved breath whispered across Alex's neck. Alex shifted Brody to his other hip, then took Tammy's hand in his own, threading his fingers through hers and tugging her close to his side.

"There's one more thing I discovered when I was completing paperwork for Brody," Maxine said, her smile growing wider. "His first birthday is at the end of next week. Saturday, to be exact. Thought I'd let you know in case you wanted to plan something special for him."

"Oh, that's perfect, Alex." Tammy grinned up at him. "With the power back on, I could make Brody a birthday cake. One of those little individual ones with lots of colorful icing. And we could blow up some balloons and get party favors—"

Alex laughed, gesturing with their joined hands toward the fields surrounding them. "And where exactly do you plan on rounding all this stuff up?"

Tammy fell silent, frowning and biting her lip.

"The grocery store in Deer Creek reopened a few days ago," Maxine said. "I'm sure you'll find most of what you need there. But you'll want to get there soon. From what I hear, the lines are stretching out of the front door, and they're already getting low on milk and bread."

Tammy's expression brightened, and she clutched the medal to her chest, her body practically vibrating against his with excitement. "How 'bout it? Want to take a trip to town?"

Not particularly. Alex rolled his shoulders and sighed. How long *had* it been since he'd actually shown his face in Deer Creek? Dean and Gloria had undertaken all the errands for the ranch, and normally he drove an hour in the opposite direction to get groceries in a different county.

He grimaced. Going to Deer Creek meant potentially bumping into old friends and classmates whose calls and visits he'd avoided for years. And he damned sure didn't relish the idea of carrying on conversations about what he'd been doing with his life since his split with Susan.

"Please, Alex. We need groceries anyway, and it'll be Brody's first birthday. He deserves to have a special day." Tammy leaned over and kissed Brody's forehead. "Don't you, handsome?"

Brody chortled, squished Tammy's cheeks with both hands and tugged her closer for more kisses. They both giggled, then glanced up at Alex with beaming smiles.

Aw, hell. The cute factor was off the charts. And he knew when he was beaten.

He chuckled. "When do you want to leave?"

It took longer than he remembered to drive into the city limits of Deer Creek, the distance seeming greater than usual. The houses and businesses in town had been damaged and there were a lot of downed trees, but the bulk of debris had been cleared from the roads, and the small business district of the community was bustling.

Maxine had definitely heard right. Two lines stretched out of the Deer Creek Market's front entrance, and the parking lot was packed.

"I think everybody and their brother are here restocking supplies." Alex eased his truck into a parking space and cut the engine. "Want to divide and conquer? Or bulldoze our way through there together?"

Tammy unsnapped her seat belt and lifted her chin. "Bulldoze our way in together." She twisted and peered into the back of the cab. "That okay with you, Brody?"

The baby squealed and kicked his feet against the car seat.

Decision made, they wove their way through the crowd, snagged a shopping cart and headed straight for the dairy section. Tammy held Brody while Alex grabbed the last two gallons of milk and a carton of eggs. Diapers and baby food were next, then they eventually made their way to the cake mix aisle.

"Mind holding him for a sec?" Tammy asked, passing Brody to Alex, then bending to inspect the various boxes.

Alex settled Brody on his hip while Tammy picked out a box of cake mix and a can of icing, tossing them in the cart. He glanced around, noticing a few curious looks from other shoppers. He shifted from one boot to the other as Tammy browsed a small selection of pans.

She poked around the items on the shelf, then held up a cupcake tin in one hand and a large griddle in the other. "Which one?"

Alex bit back a laugh. "Have you ever baked a cake before?"

She grinned sheepishly, then shrugged. "There's a first time for everything, right?" Blushing, she added firmly, "I've decided to make this a summer of firsts."

Something in her eyes provoked a strong hunger within him. One that had nothing to do with food. He waved a hand at the cart. "Throw 'em both in there. We'll figure it out together."

Together. He held the word on his tongue, relishing the feel of it. Shopping together with a woman and a baby was definitely a first for him. A first he wouldn't mind repeating with Tammy and Brody for as long as current circumstances allowed.

"We're getting a lot of interested stares," Tammy whispered, eyeing a couple craning their necks for a better glimpse as they passed. "Do I look that out of place?"

Alex shook his head. "It's not you, it's me. It's been a while since I came into town. Deer Creek is small, and news travels fast." He winced. "I haven't been all that friendly to people lately."

"Yeah." She nodded, adopting a solemn expression. "They're probably afraid of you."

He frowned, heat snaking up his neck. "Afraid?"

"Well, you are a very manly kind of man," she said, eyeing his chest and arms. "Some people might find that intimidating." Her mouth twitched. "Except for me and Brody. We know you're just a big ol' teddy bear."

As if on cue, Brody yawned, blinked heavily, then laid his cheek against Alex's chest.

Tammy laughed. "See what I mean?" She froze, then threw her hands in the air. "Oh, I forgot the balloons. We can't have a party without those. I'll be back in a minute."

And she was off, rushing down the aisle and around the corner.

Alex chuckled under his breath, then bent his head to Brody's ear and whispered, "She's got a lot more energy than either of us right now, huh, little man?"

Brody rubbed his eyes, then stuck his thumb in his mouth.

Alex smiled, lingering close to Brody's hair and breathing in his soft baby scent. The light weight of him in his arms was comforting—soothing, almost— and he couldn't help but remember how happy Dean had looked holding his son.

His chest tightened, a devoted pride swelling within him. Was this how it had been for Dean? Was this how it felt to be a father?

"Alex?"

He froze. The voice was soft. Barely discernible. But he recognized it instantly.

He lifted his head, swallowed hard and turned. "Susan."

She hadn't changed much. She still had the same thick blond hair, bright blue eyes and clear complexion. The lines beside her mouth were a bit deeper, but they just drew attention to her appealing smile. Time had been good to her.

"I…I thought it was you, but…" Her hesitant words trailed off, and she shifted restlessly behind her shopping cart as her eyes drifted down and hovered on Brody.

Alex forced a smile. "It's been a long time."

"Yes," she said softly, looking up at him again. "It has."

"You look well."

"Thank you. So do you." She glanced down, cheeks flushing. "I heard about Dean and Gloria. I'm so sorry. I know I didn't keep in touch, but I still loved them." Glancing at Brody, she bit her lip, then asked, "Is he their son?" At Alex's nod, she continued, "It's so unfair for him to have to grow up without them. I can't bear to think of my girls having to go through something like that."

His throat constricted, and it hurt to speak. "You have children?"

Susan nodded, smiling. "Three daughters. The oldest is six, and the twins are four. They're at home, helping their dad clean up the damage from the storm." Her voice weakened. "I remarried seven years ago."

"That's good. You always said you wanted a big family." He clutched Brody tighter, his voice hoarse. "I'm happy for you."

She tucked a curl behind her ear with a shaky hand, then adjusted her purse strap on her shoulder. "How about you? Still living outside town?"

Heat scorched his face. "Same place."

Her eyes glistened. "At…at our house?"

Our house. He gritted his teeth and looked away. It'd stopped being their house the day she'd asked for a divorce, crying for hours in his arms and saying she loved him but that a future without children of her own wasn't the life she'd envisioned. That adopting and being a mother to someone else's child wouldn't be enough.

And the hell of it was, he'd known it was coming. Had seen it solidifying in her eyes for months after they learned of his infertility. Before, their disappointment at being unable to conceive could be brushed aside, but once they'd discovered the possibility of a pregnancy was nonexistent, it was an issue they could no longer ignore.

"I'm sorry," she said. "I didn't mean to offend you. I thought you would've sold it after—" Her voice broke, and she moved closer. "It's just that I still think of it as our place, you know? I still think of how beautiful it was and how many good times we had." She stopped and refocused on Brody, her lower lip trembling and face paling. "I've wanted to call you for a long time. I wanted to tell you—"

"Found 'em."

Tammy's hip bumped against his. She tossed a pack of balloons in the cart, then glanced up, stilling as she noticed Susan.

"Oh." Tammy looked from Susan to him, then back again, her smile fading. "I didn't mean to interrupt."

"You're not," Alex said. His chest tightened painfully, and he struggled to soften the hard edge in his tone. "We're done. Aren't we, Susan?"

An uncomfortable silence ensued, stretching on for

what seemed like an eternity, until Susan spoke, her voice strained.

"I just wanted to tell you that I wish things had turned out differently. That I'm sorry. For everything." She backed away. "You look good holding a baby, Alex." Her smile shook and she wiped away a tear, whispering as she left, "I always imagined you would."

Alex stood still and watched her walk away. A heavy weight settled over him, weakening his body and making his arms tremble beneath Brody. And he felt like a bigger failure than ever.

"Take him." Avoiding Tammy's eyes, he pressed Brody into her arms, then grabbed the cart and shoved it to the front of the store.

He managed to make it through the long wait at the checkout, pay for the groceries and load the bags in the truck without losing his composure. He even managed to crank the engine and drive in a straight line all the way back to the ranch.

But he couldn't manage to face Tammy. Not once. Because he was too afraid to answer the questions that would inevitably come. And he couldn't stand to see the same look in her eyes that he'd seen in Susan's when she realized what a fraud he really was.

TAMMY SETTLED BRODY in the crib, then kissed his forehead. "Sleep well, sweet boy."

He made a soft sound of contentment, his thumb sliding from his mouth as he drifted off. She slipped quietly from the nursery, pausing to pet Scout, who was asleep on the floor, then walked to the kitchen and peered out the window.

Night had fallen, and the bright moon spilled a soft

white glow across the front porch, highlighting Alex's profile. He sat on the top step, his elbows propped on his knees and a liquor bottle dangling between his fingers. He had the same expression on his face that he'd maintained during the silent drive back from the Deer Creek grocery store.

Blank and unapproachable.

Tammy pulled in a deep breath and made her way onto the porch, shutting the door behind her. "Is it okay if I join you?"

His broad shoulders stiffened. He shrugged but didn't face her.

She smiled. "I'll take that as a yes."

Tammy eased down beside him on the step, laughing as she squirmed for a comfortable position. "You know, this porch would be a lot more welcoming with a couple of rocking chairs."

No response.

She motioned toward the dimly lit walls of the stable in the distance. "Sapphire and Razz were doing well when I checked on them earlier."

Alex nodded and turned away, staring at the empty fields. The stubble on his jaw had darkened, and the thick waves of his hair curled slightly at his nape.

Her fingertips tingled, wanting to slip through the soft strands, slide beneath the collar of his black T-shirt and caress his warm skin. Smooth across the thick muscles of his back and feel the tension release from his brawny frame. Anything to return the charismatic smile that had brightened his handsome face that night in the creek.

"I just put Brody to bed. He went out like a light." She bumped his shoulder with hers and grinned. "Scout did, too. You're gonna have dog hair all over the nursery carpet tomorrow morning."

He shifted away from her on the step, his guarded expression so similar to the one he'd had when she'd first arrived. He hadn't spoken a word since Susan had walked away from him in the store.

Susan. Tammy's stomach tensed. The former wife whom Alex and Maxine talked around instead of about. A woman who could cast a shadow over Alex's entire day with just a brief conversation. Tammy clasped her hands together and pressed them between her knees, wincing as she recalled the woman's words.

I wish things had turned out differently.

There'd been no mistaking that, judging from the pretty blonde's tearful expression and regretful tone. It was clear Susan still had strong feelings for Alex. But did Alex feel the same?

Her chest stung, the question a more unwelcome one than she'd expected. And one she'd give just about anything to settle for certain.

Hesitating, she gestured toward the bottle Alex held. "That stuff helping you feel better?"

He grunted, studied the bottle in his hand, then faced her. "You could say that."

Stomach churning, Tammy took a deep breath, then said, "My dad used to go through several of those things in a week, and it never seemed to solve any of his problems." Her throat thickened, and she hugged her knees to her chest. "It just made him mean."

Alex frowned, his eyes roving over her face, neck and arms.

Her skin tightened in patches where old wounds had been inflicted. She squirmed and glanced down, half expecting blotches of bruises to resurface on her flesh. Which was ridiculous.

"What does it do to you?" she asked, cringing at the weak thread in her voice.

"The whiskey?"

She nodded.

The gray depths of his eyes gentled. "It helps me forget."

"Forget Susan?" She bit her lip. "I'm sorry. It's none of my business, but…"

"But you want to know," Alex murmured, glancing back down at the bottle in his hands.

"Yeah." She held her hand out, palm up, and nudged his knee with her knuckles. "We could talk instead. And it goes both ways, you know? You could ask me anything."

He hesitated, then handed her the bottle, a small smile appearing. "Are you curious about Susan because you're jealous?"

The bottle slipped from her grasp, and she scrambled, catching it before it shattered against the brick step. "Really?" She laughed, hands shaking. "That's the first question you want to ask?"

"Yep." His smile widened. "You said anything."

Face heating, she set the bottle on the porch landing before answering, "Yes." Her heart skipped at the pleased gleam in his eyes. "I'm a little jealous."

He raised an eyebrow. "Only a little?"

"That's two questions," she said, giving him a pointed look. "It's my turn. What other jobs have you had besides ranching and breeding horses?"

"I made decent money bull riding years ago."

Her mouth dropped open. "You were a bull rider?"

He laughed. "Only briefly. And don't look so surprised. I may not have a world championship buckle, but I was able to hold my own when the occasion called for it."

"No. I mean, I wouldn't doubt that." Her eyes clung to the strong curve of his biceps, a delicious shiver running through her as she imagined his powerful frame striding across an arena. "It's just..." Lord, she was being rude. She tore her eyes away and took a deep breath. "It's just that I don't see you as the roaming type." She frowned. "Of course, I didn't think of my cousin Colt as the settling-down type, but that's what he went and did. He's managing a guest ranch in Raintree and marrying my best friend in two weeks."

Alex leaned back on his elbows, studying her. "You don't seem as excited about that as I would've expected. Weddings are usually happy occasions for most people."

"Oh, it is." Tammy smiled, excitement coursing through her veins. "I can't wait to see Colt in a tux, and I know Jen's dress will be beautiful. They're perfect for each other, and I'm happy for them." She looked down, picking at a loose thread on the hem of her jeans. "It's just that Colt was my partner. He rode bulls and I barrel raced. We toured the circuit together for years."

"Years?" Alex peered down at her. "You must've left home at a young age."

"Yeah. When I was seventeen."

"How old are you?"

"Twenty-five. You?"

He gave a wry smile. "I've got ten years on you." His smile slipped. "Why'd you leave home?"

She hesitated. "Things were rough. We didn't exactly have a model family. I didn't feel like I fit in there, and I wanted out. Colt wasn't happy where he was, either, so we packed up and took off. We met Jen on the circuit. She barrel raced, too, and joined up with us. For the longest time, we were a family of sorts, until Colt's father died. Then he and Jen retired to raise Colt's little sister and start their own family. Now I'm the only one left traveling." She shrugged. "It gets lonely on the road."

"You don't like being alone?"

She glanced up, stilling at the somber expression on his face. "No. Not at all. Do you?"

He looked away. "I didn't use to. But I began to prefer it after Susan and I divorced."

"How long were you married?"

"Two years."

Tammy studied the toes of her boots. "What happened?"

He remained silent for a moment, then said, "There were things she wanted that I couldn't give her."

"What kind of things?"

He straightened, hands clenching around the edge of the step.

"Alex?" A bigger house? Money? Tammy shook her head and slid closer, the defeated slump of his shoulders making her heart ache. "You've built a beautiful home here," she whispered. "Invested in a business that would keep you close to raise a family and spend more time together." She covered his hand with her own and squeezed. "That's the kind of life I dreamed about when I was a girl. I never had any brothers or sisters, and I always felt alone. Before racing, all I ever wanted was a peaceful home and a big family of my own to love."

He closed his eyes, and a muscle in his jaw ticked.

"When you showed me the nursery the other night,

I couldn't help but wonder if you might have lost a child—"

"No." He blew out a heavy breath then faced her. "I…" He made as if to continue, then dragged his teeth over his bottom lip, his eyes heavy and shadowed as they examined her face.

Throat aching, she asked, "Do you still love her?"

He blinked, his brow furrowing. "I fell out of love with Susan a long time ago. I've just been angry with the way things ended. With the fact that what we had wasn't enough for her. That *I* wasn't enough." He shook his head. "But it wasn't Susan's fault. She's a good person. She just wanted to be happy, and she did what she had to do to get there." His voice turned hoarse, his words strained as he repeated, "She's a good person."

Tammy cupped his face, the stubble on his jaw rasping against her fingertips. "So are you." Something heady and warm unfurled within her, dancing in her veins and urging her closer. "And you're so much more than just enough, Alex."

His eyes softened, and his throat moved beneath the heels of her hands on a hard swallow.

She leaned closer, wanting so much to prove it. To show him. To share at least a small part of the intense feelings he stirred within her. "I'm going to kiss you."

Cheeks heating, she cringed at the high-pitched uncertainty in her voice. *Great.* So much for a smooth approach.

His brows lifted, then a soft rumble of laughter escaped his lips. "Are you asking me, babe? Or telling me?"

The flirtatious tone of his voice untied the knot in her belly, and the intoxicating buzz in her veins flooded her senses, spurring her on. She moved across the step, straddling his thighs, and smiled down at him. "I'm telling you."

His mouth parted, and his gray eyes darkened as he whispered, "Well, hell. Have at it."

Head spinning, she closed her eyes and eased closer, her lips hovering a fraction of an inch above his, their rapid breaths mingling. His distinctive scent, sandalwood and man, enveloped her. Her belly heated, but her muscles tensed, her limbs turning cold and stiff.

It'd been so long since she'd taken a chance and allowed her body to be vulnerable to a man. And even then, the few fumbling kisses she'd dug up enough courage to enjoy had been fleeting at best. They were nothing like the kinds of kisses a man like Alex was probably used to.

Oh, God. What if her inexperience showed? What if she humiliated herself? In front of Alex, of all men?

"Tammy?"

She hesitated, squeezing her eyes tighter, and concentrated on the soothing sound of his voice. Her body trembled, and she struggled to relax. To let go and…

"Tammy." His voice firmed, his thighs shifting beneath her. "Are you afraid of me?"

Her eyes shot open. The teasing expression had left him, concern taking its place. "What?"

She looked down, finding her hands covering his on the step, flattening his palms hard into the brick at his sides. His fingertips were red beneath the heels of her hands.

"Are you afraid of me?" He peered up at her. "Because you've got to know, I'd never hurt you. Never."

He shook his head. "Maybe I do look intimidating to some people, but—"

"No." She released his hands, placed hers on his chest and whispered just before covering his mouth with hers, "I'm not afraid."

She wasn't. Not one bit. Even when the tang of whiskey clinging to his lips touched her tongue, she forged past it. She slid her arms around his neck, pulled him closer and searched deeper for the man she'd grown to trust and admire.

And there he was. The intoxicating taste of him just as pure and potent as the liquor. But so much more exciting and addictive. She explored him fully, easing her tongue past his lips, threading her fingers through his hair and pressing her breasts against his hard chest.

He groaned, the deep rumble vibrating against her rib cage as his big, warm palms delved beneath her shirt, gliding up her back in caressing strokes. His teeth nibbled at her lower lip, the gentle pressure sending delicious shivers down her spine. His hands drifted lower, cupping her bottom and pulling her tight against his hips.

A cry of pleasure escaped her. Tammy leaned back and looked down, absorbing his tousled hair, passion-filled eyes and kiss-reddened mouth. There were no insecurities. No anxieties. And no fears. Just a strong desire to ease back into his arms and discover just how powerful this connection between them could become.

Tammy leaned closer and rubbed the nape of his neck with her fingertips. "You're so much more than enough, Alex." She grinned, her lips brushing his ear as she whispered, "And I'm always available if you need to forget."

His broad chest jerked with laughter. He smoothed her hair from her cheeks, eyes roving over her face, then his warm mouth claimed hers, each of his hungry kisses heightening her desire.

A weight lifted from her, lightening her chest and strengthening her limbs, and she felt stronger than ever. She no longer wanted to run. What she wanted, more than anything, was to stay right in his arms.

Chapter Seven

"I may not be a decent cook," Tammy said, jerking on an oven mitt. "But I rock at icing."

Alex leaned into his elbows on the kitchen island and smiled, watching as she spun around and opened the oven to remove a pan of freshly baked cupcakes.

After three failed attempts at baking a cake and two additional trips to the Deer Creek Market for more cake mix, Tammy had finally accepted his suggestion to try making cupcakes for Brody's birthday party instead. And judging from the pleasant aroma filling the kitchen, he'd bet good money this batch was going to be...

She bent over, and the denim covering her curvy backside pulled tight, halting his thoughts and sending his blood south.

Damn. He stifled a groan and pressed his hands tight to the table, his palms tingling with the remembered feel of her soft curves filling them. It'd been a week since he'd held her in his arms on the porch and over one hundred and sixty-eight hours since he'd thoroughly kissed her. Not that he was keeping count.

The decorative stitching on her back pockets vanished, and she faced him, tipping the cupcakes in his direction.

"…together with lots of icing."

He blinked, dragged his eyes up past her tempting breasts and focused on her face. "What did you say?"

"I said we could stack a few of these on top of each other and stick them together with lots of icing." She smiled. "Then it'd at least look like a cake. Wouldn't it, Brody?"

Alex glanced over his shoulder. Brody looked up from his seated position on the floor, grinned mischievously, then banged the wooden spoons in his hands on the metal pot between his knees. Scout barked and ran around him in circles.

"Do you think he'd like blue or yellow frosting the best?" Tammy asked, yelling over the racket.

"Both."

She cupped her free hand to her ear and tilted her head. "Blue?"

"Both," Alex shouted, laughing at the chaos filling his kitchen.

Lord, it felt good. So good to laugh and talk and kiss. To have life fill his home again. He hadn't realized how empty it'd truly been until Brody and Tammy had stepped inside it.

Brody, distracted by the shiny buttons on his overalls, stopped banging the pot, tucked his chin to his chest and started picking at his straps. Scout skipped over and started gnawing Brody's untied shoelaces.

"So you think we should use the blue *and* the yellow?" Tammy asked.

"Yep," Alex said, the sight of Brody and Scout widening his smile. There wasn't a cuter kid on the planet. "I think he'd like both."

"And you were checking me out earlier, right?"

"Yeah." Alex jerked upright. "Wait, what?"

"Busted." Tammy winked, green eyes twinkling. "Not that I mind. As a matter of fact— Ouch!"

She jumped, the pan falling from her hold and clattering to the table. One cupcake bounced out and rolled across the floor. Scout darted after it, trapped it with a paw and started chomping, his loud smacks filling the kitchen. Brody cackled and banged the pot again.

Tammy jerked the oven mitt from her hand, blowing furiously on her fingers. "Doggone thing was hotter than I thought," she said, waving her hand back and forth through the air. "Burned me right through the mitt."

"Let me see." Alex walked around the island and took her hand. Bright red blotches marred her fingertips. "Here."

He tugged her to the sink, turned on the faucet, then held her fingers under the cold stream of water. She relaxed and leaned against his shoulder, the soft scent of her shampoo releasing from her hair.

He firmed his hold on her wrist, fighting the urge to drift his fingers through the shiny waves, cup the back of her head and plunder the soft curves of her mouth. "Better?"

"Mmm-hmm." She tipped her head back and looked up at him, those beautiful eyes lingering on his lips, her cheeks blushing a pretty pink.

Alex turned off the water, then lifted her hand to his mouth, kissing her fingertips. Her mouth parted, and she pressed close.

I'm always available if you need to forget.

He squeezed her hand gently, realizing he hadn't sought comfort in a bottle since that night they'd shared on the porch. He hadn't felt the need for it. Because the trouble was, he didn't want to forget anything. He wanted to remember every moment he had with Tammy. Wanted to imprint the silky feel of her skin on his hands, memorize the delightful chime of her laugh and capture every sweet sigh against his lips. And he'd had only a few brief moments over the past week to savor a quick brush of his lips over hers. The immediate needs of the ranch had taken over, preventing anything more.

Last week, two more horses, Jet and Cisco, had wandered back to the ranch in poor shape, but the vet assured Alex they'd recover given time and attention. Tammy had worked as hard as he had to heal the animals and complete repairs over the past several days. They'd spent the majority of their time caring for Brody, rehabilitating Razz and Sapphire, and restoring the stable. And Brody was beginning to recover from the loss of his parents. He hadn't cried for them in several days and he smiled more than ever.

The more time Alex spent with Tammy and Brody, the more precious they'd become. But like every valuable summer he'd spent with Dean, this one would eventually come to an end, too.

He winced, hoping their time together would last longer than he thought. Because, though he'd tried, he had difficulty envisioning his home without them. And he couldn't shake the nagging feeling that the privacy he'd craved in the past might become isolating after Tammy and Brody left.

He reached out and cradled her face with his palms, shaking off the invasive thought. He'd lived long enough to recognize an opportunity when it presented itself. Tammy was here. Right in front of him. He was going to enjoy whatever little time he had left with her and make damned sure Brody had a fantastic first birthday. The kind of birthday Dean would've wanted for his son.

Alex nudged Tammy back against the island and slipped a leg between hers. "I'm going to kiss you," he teased, angling his lips close to hers and raising his voice above Brody's banging and Scout's snuffles. He smiled, hoping the chaos didn't kill all the romance of the moment. "Right here, right now."

She laughed and half shouted, "Are you asking me or telling me?"

"Asking." He outlined her lips with his finger, a wave of need surging through him at the catch of her breath. "There's a sweet smell in the air and we've got a one-toddler band serenading us. I'm hoping that's enough to sway you."

Her green eyes softened. She wrapped her arms around his waist and tilted her mouth in invitation. "That's more than enough."

Something shifted in his chest. He touched his lips to hers, tasting and teasing, and the heat filling him intensified. It throbbed deep within him, overpowering the loud noises filling the kitchen and swelling with each of her soft sighs of pleasure.

It'd been so long since he felt it, he almost didn't recognize it. He'd forgotten how all consuming and disorienting it could become. But he knew exactly what that strong surge in his chest and deep pull in his gut meant.

He was falling in love.

He stilled, heart stalling. It'd happened so fast, he'd almost missed it. And it sure as hell wasn't a good idea. But Tammy had slipped right into his heart and had him thinking of her every day.

When he was tending to the horses and rebuilding

fences, he dreamed of holding her. When he was hauling off broken limbs and replacing windows, he imagined kissing her. And he remained fixated on thoughts of her during the hours before dawn when, after tossing and turning in the guest room, he'd slip out to the stable to sand and reapply varnish to neglected rocking chairs he'd constructed years ago.

All so he could make Brody's first birthday as special for Tammy as it would be for him. So he could enjoy more precious moments with her, rocking beside her on the front porch and sharing more kisses. And, heaven help him, moments like the one last week—and now—made him wonder if what he and Tammy shared could be real. They made him hope that the future might hold something more for him.

You're so much more than enough, Alex.

Reluctantly, he lifted his head. "I've got a surprise for you."

Her eyes opened slowly, a dazed wistfulness filling her expression. "Does it involve more kisses?"

Alex laughed, pressed one more lingering kiss to her lips, then straightened. "Lord, I hope so." He released her and crossed the kitchen to kneel in front of Brody. "Wanna help me out, birthday man?"

Brody stopped banging the pot, dropped the spoons and clambered to his feet. He smiled, then ran into Alex's arms, babbling as Alex propped him on his hip and stood. Not to be outdone, Scout followed, slipping on the tiled floor and barreling into Alex's boots.

"All right, Scout. You can come, too." He stopped midstride and frowned at the pup. "So long as you don't chew on anything."

"What about me?" Tammy asked, rounding the island.

"Mind waiting here a minute? I need to set up the surprise first. It's a beautiful day. I thought I'd set up a folding table, too, and we could have the party outside."

She nodded, mouth twitching as she stood on her tiptoes and cut her eyes toward the window. "Sure. I'll just stay here and work on the cake."

Chuckling, Alex paused on his way out to close the blinds, tossing over his shoulder, "No peeking."

It was tough moving two rocking chairs from the stable to the front porch with an adventurous one-year-old and a frisky pup in tow. But he managed it. And the bright red bows he tied to the center slats brought out the cherry undertones in the dark varnish pretty damned well, if he did say so himself.

"Pfffttt."

Alex glanced down, biting back a smile as Brody blew raspberries and shoved one of the chairs, watching with wide eyes as it rocked back and forth.

"What? You don't like 'em?"

Brody pointed at the chair and squealed.

"Oh, I get it. They're too big, huh?" Alex smiled. "Well, don't worry, birthday man. I've got you covered."

Alex jogged across the front lawn with Scout at his heels, keeping a careful eye on Brody as he retrieved a third rocking chair from the bed of his truck. This one was much smaller. He carried it to the porch, set it down carefully between the other two, then lowered to his haunches, eyeing Brody closely.

He'd never made baby furniture before. And especially not in the short amount of time that he'd had to put this one together. The measurements could be way off.

"Wanna give it a try?"

He held his breath, his lungs burning as Brody toddled

his way over, grabbed the tiny armrests and climbed up. The small chair tilted forward, and Alex grabbed it, holding it steady as Brody settled in the center.

It fit him perfectly. There was even enough extra space to ensure he could still enjoy it after growing several more inches. And Scout took full advantage, leaping into the chair and stretching out across Brody's lap.

Brody leaned forward, then sat back, rocking the chair. A wide smile broke out across his face, exposing his small teeth, and he giggled. The delighted sound morphed into full-blown laughter as he glided back and forth. The baby-fine strands of his hair ruffled in the warm afternoon breeze, and his chubby cheeks flushed with excitement.

Alex swallowed the tight knot in his throat. How many days did he have left with Brody? Maxine hadn't called with an update on the uncle's situation, and his heart broke at the idea of Brody not being claimed by a family member.

But when it came down to it…wasn't *he* family? He'd been Dean's best friend and had vicariously lived every monumental moment in Brody's life so far through Dean. And he'd helped Brody survive the most devastating time in his life *without* Dean and Gloria. Didn't that count for something?

Alex tightened his grip on the chair, hope swelling in his chest. When Maxine had first asked him to take Brody in, he couldn't imagine being able to scrape by as a decent guardian. But now, he found himself wanting the chance to try. If he was given a shot, he'd do everything he could to make sure Brody was provided for and protected. More than that. He'd make sure Brody knew he was loved.

Hell, he knew how it felt not to be wanted. He'd never had a real family of his own as a child, and after his failed marriage, Dean and Gloria had been the closest he'd ever come to having one as an adult. Dean and Gloria had loved and wanted Brody before he was even born—Brody had never known anything different—and it damned near broke Alex's heart to think Brody could possibly lose that feeling.

Alex gently covered Brody's hand on the chair with his. He'd never be a father in the truest sense of the word. He'd accepted that. But if he asked, could Maxine find a way for him to keep Brody? And if he had Brody, he might be able to give Tammy some of what she wanted. At least enough to make her happy and tempt her to stay.

Would life actually deal in his favor for once and give him another shot at building a home with a child who needed him? And a woman he loved?

The strength of emotion spearing through Alex made it difficult to speak. He brushed a kiss across the baby's forehead and whispered, "Happy birthday, Brody."

A soft gasp sounded. Tammy stepped onto the porch, her hand covering her mouth and her gaze fixed on Brody.

Alex bit back a grin. "You were supposed to wait."

Her eyes met his, glistening in the sunlight, as she lowered her hand. "I couldn't wait any longer. Not after hearing Brody laugh like that." She walked over and trailed her fingers over the back of one of the chairs. Her touch lingered on the decorative edges. "You made these?"

He nodded. "Two of them I made a long time ago. They were the only items in the stable that made it through the storm virtually untouched. They just needed to be refinished. I made Brody's over the past week."

She shook her head, smiling. "They're gorgeous, Alex."

Brody yelped, slapped his hands on his armrests, then babbled up at Tammy.

"I think he wants you to try it out." Alex stood and gestured toward the chair. "Go ahead."

She rounded the chair, sat down, then smoothed her hands appreciatively over the armrests. Alex sat in the third rocking chair on the other side of Brody.

"Someone told me this porch would be more welcoming with rocking chairs," he said. "You think these fit the bill?"

Tammy leaned her head against the headrest and smiled. "They're perfect."

He eased back in his chair, the sight of pleased surprise on her face making the extra hours of hard work more than worth it. He pushed Brody's chair gently and helped him rock. Tammy did the same, and they sat for several minutes, enjoying the sight of Razz and Sapphire grazing in the green field, absorbing the beauty of the summer day and savoring Brody's enjoyment.

Alex closed his eyes, listening to Tammy's gentle teasing and Brody's responding laughter. How great it would be to end a long day of hard work like this. Hell, he could tough out any backbreaking project if he knew he'd see Tammy smile and hear Brody laugh at the start and end of each day. And what was most surprising was that the idea no longer felt out of reach.

"That's not Ms. Maxine or Earl, is it?" Worry laced Tammy's tone. "I told them we'd start the party at three, and it's only a little after one."

Alex opened his eyes and glanced at the driveway. Sunlight glared off a vehicle as it approached, and dust billowed out behind it.

"I haven't finished the cake yet," Tammy said. "Or put up the decorations…"

The growl of the engine drew closer.

"That's not Earl," Alex said, squinting at the approaching shape. "He comes in on the back road. It's not Maxine, either. She drives one of those compacts. That's a—"

"Truck," Tammy shouted, jumping to her feet, her voice pitching higher with excitement. "*My* truck." She darted down the porch steps and across the lawn, spinning back briefly to call out, "*And* Razz's trailer."

Alex froze. His boots glued to the porch floor, and his chair jerked to a halt.

Tammy ran to the driveway, waited until the truck stopped, then hopped onto the running board. Her breathless voice carried across the yard as she talked to the driver, her laughter ringing out occasionally.

Brody grunted and pointed at Tammy. His fingers curled in midair as if to pull her to him, then he looked up at Alex and frowned.

"I know," Alex mumbled, a hollow forming in his gut.

Tammy could go anywhere now. To her friends' ranch for the wedding, back to the circuit to resume racing and, eventually, to Vegas to win a new championship. The whole world lay at her feet. His battered ranch was merely a bedraggled speck on an otherwise pristine map. And it would be selfish and unfair to ask her to sacrifice her dreams.

His skin chilled. "Looks like summer may be over sooner than I thought."

A BIRTHDAY JUST wasn't a birthday without a cake.

Tammy walked outside to the table Alex had set up, placed the colorful concoction she held in front of Brody and grinned. "The birthday cake has arrived."

Alex, Maxine and Earl, all seated around the table, clapped, then leaned in for a closer look.

Tammy laughed. Well, the iced-together cupcakes could pass as a cake. Of sorts. The lopsided lump was colorful, arranged into the shape of a number one, and she and Alex had even managed to write Happy Birthday, Brody, in green frosting, having mixed the blue and yellow for an added wow factor. Of course, due to limited space, the words squished together and ran slightly off the edges. But Brody didn't seem to mind. He dug his pointer finger deep into the *H* and cackled.

"Now, hold on a minute, birthday boy," Tammy teased, tugging his finger from the pile of heavily iced cupcakes. "We've got to sing first."

"Aw, let him have a taste." Alex reached across the table and scooped a bit of icing onto his fingertip.

Scout jumped at Brody's side, his ears flopping and black eyes emerging above the table as he struggled in vain to reach Alex's hand.

Brody stared at Alex's finger as it drew near. He latched on to it with both hands, brought it to his mouth and pulled off the icing. His brown eyes widened, then he licked his lips and squealed.

"What'd I tell you?" Tammy asked, smiling at Alex. "I rock at icing."

Alex laughed, then grabbed a napkin and looked down, his smile fading as he wiped his hands.

Tammy retrieved the yellow bib Maxine had brought and fastened it loosely around Brody's neck, then glanced at Alex. He'd grown quiet again. He'd smiled and played with Brody as they'd assembled the cake and put up decorations, but the flirtatious demeanor from two hours ago had dimmed. It'd started slipping away as soon as her truck had appeared in the driveway. And he'd become even more guarded since Maxine and Earl had arrived.

"All right, y'all," Earl bellowed, leaning forward in his lawn chair and sharing a smile with Maxine. "That boy's hungry. Let's do this on the count of three."

Earl counted them off, then everyone joined in for a less-than-stellar performance of "Happy Birthday." Scout howled. Brody's gaze darted over each of them, fixating on their mouths, and he bounced in his high chair, gurgling with excitement.

When they finished, Alex nudged the makeshift cake closer to Brody. "It's all yours, little man."

Brody looked down at the cake, smiled up at Alex, then dived face-first into it, his fists gripping the sides as he mouthed the icing. Clumps of blue and yellow frosting plopped onto the table as he jerked upright, giggling and flexing his cake-coated fingers.

His delight was infectious, and everyone laughed.

"Everything's beautiful, Tammy." Maxine smiled, gesturing toward the colorful streamers and balloons taped to the tablecloth. "You and Alex have really outdone yourselves."

"Thanks." Tammy shrugged, sat down and sipped her soda. "I just wish I had a better touch in the kitchen. The cake didn't turn out quite like I wanted."

"Oh, you did a fine job," Maxine said.

"Better than fine." Alex pinched off a piece and popped it into his mouth. "It's delicious."

Brody chortled, then reached up and patted Alex's

face, smearing cake crumbs all over his jaw. Chuckling, Alex leaned over and placed noisy kisses on Brody's messy cheeks as the baby giggled and squealed. Alex pulled away and smiled, his strong jaw and sexy mouth speckled with icing.

Tammy's heart turned over. Gracious, he was handsome. And if she imagined it just right, she could picture what he'd look like as a groom at a wedding reception. She could see him patiently posing for pictures in a tux, feel the tender press of his hand on hers as they cut the cake and taste the sweetness of his icing-laced kiss as they shared the first slice.

Her grip tightened around the plastic cup in her hand, the icy condensation a shock against her hot palm. *A wedding.* Oh, Lord. Jen and Colt's wedding was next Saturday, which meant she needed to get back on the road first thing Friday morning if she wanted to make the rehearsal on time.

But that would mean leaving Alex and Brody. Her belly fluttered. Unless, of course, she asked Alex to go with her.

She smiled, the thought of walking in on Alex's arm warming her cheeks. What she wouldn't give to spend a romantic evening with him. To meet his eyes across the aisle, brush against him during a dance and kiss him freely again beneath the stars. And she didn't want it to end there.

Was this the same feeling that had lured Jen away from the circuit and into Colt's arms? Tammy studied Alex and Brody closer, her chest tingling at the happiness on their faces. It must've been, because as much as Tammy loved to race, she loved being with Alex and Brody more.

Love. Her heart skipped. She loved Alex. And fantasizing about marrying him and staying at the ranch permanently made her ache with need. She yearned to lie beside him at night and wake up next to him every morning. To have Brody with them every day so they could laugh and play and help him grow strong. And what she dreamed of most of all was to watch her belly swell with Alex's child.

Her breath caught as she studied him. Would a baby they made have his smile or hers?

"I'm so grateful to you both."

Tammy started at the sound of Maxine's voice, the soda sloshing over the rim of the cup and trickling down her wrist.

Maxine studied Brody, smiling as he laughed. "The two of you have really made this a special day for Brody." She placed a hand on Alex's arm. "Dean and Gloria would be so happy."

Alex's cheeks flushed. He grabbed a napkin and wiped the icing from his face. "I hope so." He cleared his throat, then asked in a low voice, "Have you heard anything more from Dean's brother?"

Maxine averted her eyes and picked at the cookie on her plate. "Not yet." She sighed. "John is so young. And he's just starting out in life. I'm not sure how willing he and his fiancée are to take on an instant family. Especially since he and Dean weren't close. He barely knew Dean."

"*I* knew Dean," Alex said. "And I know Brody."

Tammy stilled. The strained note in Alex's voice and determined look in his eyes made her long to hold him close.

"I know," Maxine said quietly.

"What will happen if John doesn't come through?" Tammy asked.

"The children's home in Atlanta would be the next step."

Alex propped his elbows on the table and leaned closer. "But what if someone in Deer Creek was willing to take him?"

Maxine hesitated, exchanging a glance with Earl, then said gently, "We're not there yet, Alex. We'll have to wait on John's answer first."

Alex moved to speak but turned back to Brody, remaining silent.

Tammy placed her cup on the table, her hand trembling as she studied the tight set of Alex's jaw. He'd grown so close to Brody. They both had. It was clear he was as uncomfortable with letting Brody go as she was, and his kiss earlier made her believe he might actually feel as strongly for her as she did for him. But it was hard to tell for sure.

Which left her with only one option—to cowgirl up and show him what she wanted. To prove to him how good they could be together and ask if the future she envisioned was the kind he wanted, too. And Jen's wedding would be the perfect opportunity to make her move. If he'd just let her stay long enough to persuade him into going with her.

Tammy straightened, her spirits lifting. "All right." She stood and rubbed her hands together, suddenly eager for a moment alone with Alex. "How about we help the birthday boy open a few presents?"

Two hours later, Brody was clean, happy and sprawled in his crib, snoring with abandon. Maxine and Earl had kissed Brody's cheek, said their goodbyes, then left.

Tammy and Alex waved as they drove away, then started cleaning up the party decorations and tossing away the clumps of cake Brody had dropped.

Or rather, what was left of it. Tammy grinned, spotting Scout asleep under her newly repaired truck. The pup had done a pretty good job of gobbling up every cake crumb that had hit the ground.

"I don't think you'll need to feed Scout for a while." Tammy laughed. "His belly is probably about to pop from all that cake."

Alex smiled and pulled the plastic tablecloth off the table. "I suspect you're right about that."

She grabbed a trash bag, peeled it apart and held it open as Alex shoved the tablecloth into it. "I wasn't expecting the auto body shop to deliver my truck. I thought they'd just call and tell me it was ready."

Alex's hands stilled, then he moved away, tilted the small table on its side and folded in the legs.

"They even gave it a good wash job before they chauffeured it out to me," she added.

"Sam always did go the extra mile. He's a good guy." Alex set the folded table aside and started gathering up bits of ripped wrapping paper off the grass. "And I'm sure you're eager to get back to racing."

He smiled, but it seemed forced and died quickly.

Tammy shrugged. "I guess." She tightened her grip on the trash bag. *Ask me. Please ask me to stay.* "Getting the truck back now worked out really well because Jen's wedding is next Saturday. So I won't have to bum a ride from you."

He walked over, tossed the wrapping paper in the trash bag, then took it from her. "Why don't you take a break? I'll finish this up."

No hug. No kiss. Not even another attempt at a dimpled smile. He just turned and walked off.

Heart pounding, she stared at his broad back, watching him move farther away, then blurted out, "Can I stay?"

He stopped, the bag bumping his thigh as he stilled. "What did you say?"

"I asked if I could stay." Her voice shook, and she balled her fists at her sides. "With you and Brody. For just a little longer? I know that wasn't part of the deal, but I don't want to go just yet." Throat tightening, she forced out, "Can I stay until at least the end of next week? And then maybe…"

Alex dropped the bag, turned around and started toward her, his long strides fast and powerful.

"And then maybe we could—"

His mouth covered hers, silencing her words. His tongue parted her lips, his big hands cupped her face and his fingers speared into her hair. He filled her senses, his familiar spicy scent surrounding her and his warm, delicious taste sweeping across her tongue.

She wrapped her arms around his waist, slid her hands up to spread across his muscular shoulders, then tugged him closer. The hard length of his body aligned with hers, and she pressed against him, moaning softly.

He lifted his head and stared down at her, their heavy breaths mingling as his calloused palms caressed her nape.

"And then maybe we could all go to the wedding together," Tammy said, head spinning and body tingling. "It'd be a shame for me to go alone, seeing as how I'm maid of honor and all."

A slow smile spread across his face, and he dipped

his head, his facial stubble tickling her cheek as he kissed her more thoroughly.

She giggled breathlessly in between kisses. "Is that a yes?"

Alex smiled wider, his teeth bumping her lips gently as he whispered, "That's a hell yes."

Chapter Eight

Tammy straightened in the passenger seat of her truck, tried to still her bouncing knees and peered at the sun-drenched road ahead. A dirt driveway emerged on the right, curving through an unending stretch of green fields.

"There it is." Tammy drummed her hands on the dashboard, pointed at the road, then smiled at Alex. "Right there. Raintree Ranch."

Alex laughed, his gray eyes teasing and hands sliding farther up the steering wheel. "Are you sure? We're about an hour earlier than we expected. Maybe the turn is farther down—"

"Nope. That's the turn." Tammy unsnapped her seat belt. "We just made good time." She twisted, stretched over Brody's rear-facing car seat in the back of the cab and tapped the toe of his sneakers. "Tell him to take the turn, Brody. We're ready to see Jen and Colt, aren't we?"

Brody looked up and grinned as her hair brushed his cheek, his nose wrinkling and baby teeth appearing.

Tammy spun back around and craned her neck as Alex turned onto the dirt path. A rustic wooden sign etched with Raintree Ranch appeared, making her heart pound. Familiar white fencing lined the fields on both sides of the road, and the white, multistoried guesthouse at the end of the driveway looked as welcoming as ever.

Gracious, she was excited to see Jen. Even though she'd heard her voice a thousand times over the phone, it'd been more than a year since she'd seen her best friend in person. And Jen was getting married. To Colt. *Tomorrow!*

"Oh, you're gonna love them, Alex." Tammy wrapped her hands around Alex's brawny arm. "Jen is so easy-going and fun. And Colt is—"

She bit her lip, her stomach flipping. *Overprotective.*

Alex glanced at her and smiled, then turned his attention back to the road. "Colt is what?"

"He's…" Guarded? No. Suspicious? Uh-uh. "He's my cousin."

Alex laughed. "I know."

"Yeah. But what I mean is, we've been through a lot together." She smoothed her thumb over Alex's biceps, concentrating on his warm skin below his sleeve. "So he worries about me, you know?" She shrugged. "Like any good cousin would."

"So what you're really trying to say is that I should be prepared for the third degree."

"No. Not at all." She pulled in a deep breath. "Just don't be surprised if he asks some questions." Her grip on him tightened. "And don't let him…" Oh, Lord. *Run you off.* "Just don't read anything into it, okay? Please?"

"Relax, Tammy." He squeezed her knee. "I can handle myself."

The tight knot in the back of her neck released, her shoulders relaxing and a smile stretching her cheeks. "I know."

And it felt wonderful. So wonderful to have him by

her side and in her life. His strength and support made her feel secure in ways she never had before.

"That someone you know?" Alex asked, gesturing ahead as he drew the truck to a halt.

A tall woman ran down the front steps of the main house and darted across the front yard, her red hair streaming behind her.

"Jen!" Tammy shoved the door open, hopped out and ran.

"It's about time," Jen shouted, laughing.

"We're an hour earlier than I told you we'd be." Tammy winced as Jen hugged her tight, squeezing the air from her lungs.

"I know, but it feels like it's been years since I've seen you."

Tammy laughed as Jen's hair tickled her nose and her vision blurred. "It has. It's been a whole entire year." She pulled back, the tears rolling down Jen's cheeks making hers flow more freely. "I've missed you so much."

"Oh, you have no idea how much I've missed you." Jen dragged the backs of her hands over her cheeks, then smiled. "But you're here now."

Tammy grabbed her hands and squeezed, whispering, "And you're getting married."

Jen tipped her head back, her smile beaming as she squealed to the heavens, "I'm getting married."

"To me, I hope."

Tammy glanced over Jen's shoulder at the familiar deep voice. Her smile grew wider as Colt walked up and spun Jen around for a kiss. They shared soft whispers and a laugh, then Colt edged around Jen and wrapped his arms around Tammy.

Tammy closed her eyes and hugged him back, realizing she missed him more than she'd thought.

"I'm glad you're safe, girl," Colt said, easing back. "We were worried about you, and it's nice to finally have you here in one piece."

Tammy ruffled a hand through his blond hair, noting the relieved gleam in his blue eyes. "You think I'd let a silly tornado keep me from your wedding? I wouldn't miss it for the world."

Colt's eyes drifted over her shoulder. "Wanna introduce us?"

Tammy turned to find Alex approaching, Brody babbling in his arms. "Of course." She moved to the side, mumbling, "And I like him, so be nice."

Colt cocked an eyebrow, his grin turning mischievous. "When am I ever *not* nice?"

She gave him one last look of warning, then faced Alex. "Alex, I'd like you to meet my cousin Colt."

Alex smiled, adjusted Brody in his arms, then held out his hand. "Congratulations on your marriage."

"Thanks." Colt shook his hand. "And thanks for helping Tammy out. She told us you've been taking good care of her."

"She's done the same for me." Alex's eyes met hers, the warm gleam in them sending a delicious thrill through her.

"Tammy!"

A door slammed, then a blonde girl, around ten years old, rushed over and barreled into Tammy's middle. Tammy hugged her close, then kissed the top of her head.

"And this," Tammy said, smiling at Alex, "is Colt's

sister, Meg. Who," she teased, "I haven't seen in way too long."

Far too long, actually. Since before Meg and Colt had lost their father, prompting Colt and Jen to leave the circuit to take care of her.

"Guess what?" Meg asked. "I get to be the flower girl tomorrow. And…" She held up her hands and wiggled her fingers. "Me and Jen got matching French manicures."

"That's wonderful." Tammy studied Meg's bright expression and cheerful smile. Clearly, she was happy with Colt and Jen and it was good to see that.

"You brought a baby." Meg smiled, her blue eyes landing on Brody. "Oh, what a cutie," she crooned, easing over and taking Brody's hand.

Brody looked down at Meg and grinned as his brown eyes roved over her curls.

The rest of the introductions were made, and it wasn't long before Meg led Brody to the main house, holding his hand and laughing at his babbles the entire way.

"You decided not to bring Razz?" Jen asked.

"Yeah." Tammy studied the horses grazing in the fields. "She loves it here, but she likes it at Alex's ranch just as much. And since she's still healing, one of Alex's neighbors agreed to tend to her and the other horses for us while we're gone."

"Well, that's good." Jen smiled. "With so much family around, we have plenty of babysitters, so you and Alex can make this a sort of mini vacation. We set y'all up in two guest rooms in the main house. They're right beside each other, and if you need anything, don't hesitate to ask." She grabbed Tammy's arm and tugged. "But before you get settled, I want you to see the new house Colt had built."

"It's finished?"

"Yep." Jen laughed and pulled harder. "It's on a back lot, and I can't wait to show it to you. Colt and I just finished decorating Meg's room and found the most adorable bedroom suite. Oh, and I can show you my dress."

"Well, that officially counts me out, seeing as how I'm not allowed to see the dress before the wedding," Colt said, smirking.

"It's a surprise," Jen stressed. "I want to knock your socks off when you see me tomorrow."

"You already knock my socks off, baby." Colt winked. "And whatever you wear, you won't be wearing it for long, anyway."

Jen blushed bright red and grinned. Alex chuckled.

Tammy smacked Colt's arm playfully. "Behave."

Colt laughed, then nudged Alex with an elbow. "I say we hang here and I'll give you a hand with the bags."

Alex agreed, and Tammy and Jen left them to it, then walked the long, winding path to the back lot. The grounds at Raintree Ranch were extensive, and the new two-story house with white siding contrasted beautifully with the lush green fields surrounding it. Jen led the way inside, then through a tour of both floors. Each room they entered was even more impressive than the one before.

"I love it," Tammy said, following Jen into the master bedroom.

"I was hoping you would." Jen paused at the threshold of the closet and smiled. "Colt and I miss you. We want you to feel at home so you'll visit more often. And one day, when you're ready to retire from the circuit, maybe you'll decide to stay?" She walked inside the closet, saying over her shoulder, "But no pressure or anything."

Tammy sat on the edge of the bed and rubbed her hands over her jeans. A month ago, she'd have seriously considered the offer. She might have even decided to stay after visiting for the wedding, since the thought of returning to the road on her own was so unwelcome. But she no longer felt alone. Instead, Alex's ranch had begun to feel like home.

"Okay. Please be honest and let me know exactly what you think."

Tammy looked up as Jen walked out of the closet, holding a dress in her arms. It was off-the-shoulder white satin and the intricate detail of the lace trim was eye-catching and ornate. Soft, oversize bows adorned the off-the-shoulder sleeves and waist, giving it a gentle, romantic air.

"It's fancier than I'd originally planned," Jen said softly, ducking her head to study the dress. Her long red curls spilled over the white satin, and her cheeks flushed. "But when I saw it, I just fell in love with it."

Tammy's throat tightened, and she blinked back tears. Jen looked every inch the beautiful, blushing bride.

"It's perfect," Tammy said. "Absolutely perfect."

Jen lifted her head and smiled. "I'm glad you think so, because I picked something out for you, too."

Tammy shook her head, laughing, as Jen darted back into the closet, then returned with a second dress. "You're the bride. You should be the one getting the gifts."

"It's a gift just having you here." Jen draped a Western-style teal bridesmaid dress over her lap. "I hope you're the same size you were last year, because that's what I went by. I thought it'd bring out your eyes, and you can wear a pair of my dressy boots if you want. They'll be more comfortable than heels."

Tammy smoothed her fingers over the soft material, the white embroidery around the waist blurring in front of her. "It's beautiful. Thank you." She glanced up. "I'm so sorry I haven't been here to help, Jen."

"Oh, don't worry about that." Jen sat beside her on the bed and leaned against her. "You were needed elsewhere, and I've had more than enough help. It's going to be a simple outdoor service with family and friends. It's what Colt and I both wanted. I'm just glad you called to say you were bringing Alex and Brody with you this weekend." She laughed. "I've been itching to lay my eyes on Alex and see if he's been treating you right. And I have to say, that man is easy on a girl's eyes. I can see why you're so attracted to—"

"I'm in love with him."

Jen grew quiet, a small smile appearing as her brown eyes examined Tammy's face. "I kinda picked up on that."

Stomach fluttering, Tammy looked down and twisted her hands together in her lap. "I'm going to tell him this weekend." She cleared her throat. "I'm crazy, right? I know we haven't known each other that long and it's hard to explain, but when I'm with him, I feel like I've come home. Like I finally made a right turn somewhere and I'm meant to be there." Her hands clenched tighter, her fingertips turning red. "I want Alex so much, Jen. I want to marry him. Have children with him. Grow old with him. Life has been rough on him, and I want to see him happy," she whispered. "I want to be the one who makes him happy."

Jen's hands covered hers, squeezing gently. "I need to ask one thing."

Tammy raised her head and bit her lip at the somber look on Jen's face. "What?"

"Does he make *you* happy?"

Tammy pulled in a deep breath, sat up straight and nodded. "Yes. More than anything."

Jen smiled. "Then that's all that matters."

BRODY WAS OFFICIALLY in hog heaven.

Alex sat back in his seat and smiled as Meg, seated at a table in front of him, bounced Brody in her lap and sweet-talked him into another giggle. She hadn't let Brody out of her sight or her arms since they'd arrived at Raintree hours earlier. And the other five children seated at the kids' table seemed to enjoy Brody's company as much as she did.

"You're such a big, beautiful boy," Meg crooned above the happy chatter in Raintree Ranch's dining room.

She dipped another slice of strawberry in chocolate sauce, then handed it to him. Brody brought the strawberry to his lips with both hands, then looked across the candlelit table at Alex and smiled a toothy grin. Something about the lift of the baby's eyebrows and smug expression hinted that Brody knew exactly what he was doing.

Soft lips touched Alex's ear. "Don't tell Meg, but I think Brody's milking this rehearsal dinner for all the chocolate he can get."

Alex laughed and turned his head, his lips brushing

against Tammy's smooth cheek. "I think you're right about that."

She smothered a laugh and eased closer to his side at the head table.

The press of her breasts against his upper arm and the sweet scent of her skin sent pleasurable shivers up his spine. He raised his arm and settled it around her shoulders, leaning back to get a clearer view of her.

Damn, she was beautiful. And if the golden flicker of candlelight highlighting her deep green eyes didn't prove that fact, then the tempting curve of her smiling mouth did.

Unable to resist, he lowered his head for a quick taste of her. The hum of voices and clang of dishes in the background rose, and she moaned as he kissed her, prompting him to leave her lips and trail chaste kisses down the graceful sweep of her neck.

Her hands cradled the back of his head, and her fingertips smoothed through his hair, making his body tighten.

"What I wouldn't give to get you alone right now," she whispered, hugging him close.

"Hmm." He lifted his head, nipped her earlobe gently, then smiled as she shivered against him. "And what exactly would you do with me?"

She moved her hands to cup his jaw, her thumbs sweeping over his lower lip and those gorgeous eyes darkening. "Everything."

Sweet heaven. He dropped his head, rolled his forehead against hers and groaned. Why the hell did they have to have an audience? They'd had one earlier, too, during the wedding rehearsal outside. Tammy had looked so perfect at the end of the aisle, standing beside Jen and smiling as the sun set at her back. It'd taken all his control to keep from walking over and taking her into his arms. And even then, he hadn't been able to tear his eyes away from her.

"Excuse me."

The clink of metal against glass forced Alex to draw back to a respectable distance. He shared a regretful glance with Tammy, then focused on the dark-haired man standing at the other end of the head table. Dominic Slade. Alex remembered meeting him earlier.

After stowing the bags in the guest rooms, Colt had given Alex a tour of Raintree Ranch and introduced him to several of Tammy's friends, including Dominic. Dominic owned Raintree Ranch and was a former bull rider and traveling partner of Colt's. Everyone Alex had met had been kind and hospitable, and it was easy to see why Tammy loved this place so much.

The room grew quiet, and Dominic stopped tapping the wineglass. "As best man, I understand it's my job to give a toast and say a few words to the groom." He grinned. "And I bet Colt's shaking in his boots right now at what I'm about to say."

Scattered laughs filled the room, and Colt smiled, sitting back and curling an arm around Jen.

"No worries, though." Dominic bent and kissed the cheek of a pretty blonde sitting next to him. "My wife has given me strict instructions to keep it short and sweet." He straightened and faced Colt. "Colt, we spent a lot of years on the road together, and you've been a great business partner and even better friend."

Alex looked down, a heaviness settling in his chest. The moment felt so familiar. He could still see Dean standing in a similar pose, raising a glass and wishing

him and Susan well the night before their wedding.
Dean and Gloria had been so happy and hopeful. So
certain the future held nothing but wonderful things
for all of them.

Tammy's hand covered his, her fingers threading
through his and squeezing gently. His throat thickened,
and he focused on the contrast of her creamy skin against
his tanned hand.

"The only thing in life as valuable as a good friend is
family," Dominic continued, "and you've become that,
as well. I couldn't be happier that you've decided to
make Raintree Ranch your home." He raised his glass.
"I wish you and Jen a life full of laughter and love."
He chuckled. "And a houseful of rascals as wild as we
were as kids." He gestured toward the children's table,
his laughter trailing away and his smile wide as he said,
"Because family is what it's all about."

Alex stiffened. He glanced up and studied Tammy's
face. Her attention was fixed on the children, her eyes
shining and her lips parting. She faced him then, and
her hand tightened around his as she smiled.

He forced a smile in return, his gut churning.

Dominic raised his glass. "To Colt and Jen."

The other adults followed suit, sipped their drinks,
then applauded. After dinner concluded, friends and
family stopped by the head table to give their final congratulations before the big event. Tammy stayed close
by Alex's side.

The sheer happiness on her face was a blessing, but the
expectant adoration in her eyes was a curse. He cringed.
He knew he should tell her. Had to at some point if what
they shared turned out to be real and they decided to plan
for the future. But the rich life of family, children and a

thriving estate that lay ahead of Colt and Jen made his potential offer of a barren home and struggling ranch pale in comparison.

So much so, that even after Meg brought him Brody, the warmth of the boy's small hands hugging his neck couldn't fight the chill that had crept over Alex's skin.

One hour later, Alex stood on the front porch of the main house, holding Brody as he slept. The night sky was clear, the air was warm and the hum of nocturnal wildlife surrounded him. Tammy, Jen and Colt chatted at his side, enjoying a few moments of privacy from the crowd in the dining room.

Alex rolled his shoulders and ran a palm over Brody's hair, but the unease shrouding him refused to dissipate.

"A few of the ranch hands checked the tents earlier, and everything looks ready for tomorrow's reception," Colt said. "The food is well in hand, the decorations are up and there's nothing but sun in the weather forecast." He tugged Jen to his side and smiled. "All that's left is for you to show up, baby."

"As though I wouldn't," Jen teased, kissing his cheek.

Colt nuzzled her neck. "Why don't we just grab the preacher and do this thing now?"

"No way." Tammy poked Colt in the chest. "Jen's got a killer dress, and I refuse to leave here without seeing you in a tux. There's no telling when the opportunity will arrive again. Plus, Dominic and I have planned parties for both of you tonight. Separately," she stressed. "So say your goodbyes now."

Colt cast Alex a sardonic scowl. "You hear that, man? I'm being banished from my own home."

Alex laughed.

"You're not being banished from your home, Colt."

Tammy shrugged. "Just to the opposite side of the ranch." She moved close and rubbed Brody's back. "That means you, too, Alex. Jen's mom is babysitting tonight so we can celebrate with Jen and Colt."

Alex stifled a grin. "Separately?"

"Yep. After the party, I'm going to sleep at Jen's new house." Her smile grew brighter. She raised to her toes and whispered in his ear, "Tomorrow night, however, is another story."

Alex's mouth longed to cover hers and he leaned closer, the tension in his muscles relaxing slightly. Resisting the urge to turn his head and kiss her, he passed Brody into her waiting arms, holding a hand to the baby's head until he snuggled securely against her chest.

"I'll see you tomorrow afternoon," she said before walking inside with Brody.

Alex watched her leave, then averted his eyes and smiled as Jen shared a long good-night kiss with Colt. Reluctantly, Jen left, too.

Colt sagged back against the porch rail, pressed his palm to his chest and winced. "Damn, I love that woman."

Alex laughed.

"All jokes aside," Colt said, leaning back on his elbows. "I love Jen more than I ever thought it was possible to love someone. I can't wait to watch her walk down that aisle to me tomorrow." He shook his head and sighed. "Tonight has a strange feel to it, you know? I'm excited and nervous and eager and afraid." He laughed. "I'm feeling damned near everything. It's just…bittersweet, somehow. Having something end and begin at the same time. You know what I mean?"

Alex nodded, recalling the way his hands shook and stomach rolled the night before his wedding to Susan. He'd had all the usual nerves he'd been told to expect. But, as it turned out, his worries regarding a successful marriage hadn't been entirely unfounded.

"Yeah," he said. "I know what you mean."

Colt straightened, his smile fading. "You've done this before?"

Alex glanced away and studied the fields in the distance, the light from the porch reaching the fences, then dying a few feet past them. "Once." His mouth twisted. "Obviously, it didn't work out."

"I'm not one to judge." Colt braced a hand on the white column at his side and dragged his boot over the porch floor. "I spent a lot of time on the road and wasted a lot of years on relationships that didn't matter. Took a long time for me to get it through my thick skull that settling down was what I really wanted."

The determined note in his voice brought Alex's eyes back to him.

"The thing is, despite all of what I'm feeling now, I don't have any doubts," Colt said. "Not a single one. I love Jen, and I know this is exactly what I want. And I know marrying her is the right thing to do. For both of us."

A knot formed in Alex's gut, tightening and twisting. He stood still and waited as Colt examined his face.

"Can I be straight with you?"

Alex nodded, shoved his hands in his pockets and rocked back on his heels. "Shoot."

"How old are you?"

"Thirty-five."

Colt tapped his thumb against the column, his eyes narrowing. "Tammy is twenty-five."

"I know."

"How well would you say you know her?"

Alex frowned. "What do you mean?"

"How much has she told you about her past?"

"Not much," Alex said. "But enough."

"Enough to know she's been through some stuff?" Colt pressed.

"Yes." Alex blew out a heavy breath. "Look, I get that you're watching out for her—"

"But you want me to mind my own business?" Colt grinned, but it faded. "Tammy has been my business since the day she called eight years ago and asked me for help. Said her dad was worse than usual and she was done. That she needed to leave. I drove for hours in the middle of the night to pick her up, and when I got there, he'd beaten her so badly she could barely walk to the truck on her own." His throat moved on a hard swallow, and he jerked his chin to the side, his knuckles paling against the column. "But she made it. She picked herself up and moved on." He shook his head. "We were both kids back then. Still teenagers. And I think just the fact that I showed up that day made me her hero." He dipped his head, his blue eyes firm. "That is, until you came along."

Alex flinched, a sharp pain shooting through his palms as his nails dug into them. He uncurled his fists in his pockets, his gut roiling.

"It's tough letting go of a gig like that once you've got it—being a hero and all," Colt said. "Tammy might be my cousin, but I love her like a sister. She's been running for most of her life, and when she does decide to stay put, I want to be sure she's getting the life she deserves. The very best. And that the man she settles with cares about her as much as I do."

Something strong waved through Alex. It pushed past his chest and escaped his mouth before he realized it. "I do care for her. I love her."

"Enough to do the right thing?" Colt held his gaze. "To make her happy? Whatever it takes?"

Alex nodded. "Yes."

He said the word. And he meant it. But he prayed, even as it left him, that luck would be on his side for once. That he'd actually have a shot at giving Tammy the future and happiness she deserved.

Chapter Nine

"Smile."

Tammy knelt beside a table and squinted, eyeing Alex and Brody through the viewfinder of a disposable camera. Brody bounced in Alex's lap and grinned, his cake-coated fingers pausing on the way to his mouth. Alex looked up and smiled, bits of icing clinging to his lower lip where Brody had fed him wedding cake moments before.

Her heart turned over in her chest. *Perfect.*

"Hold it right there." She pressed the button, then nodded at the resulting click. "This one's gonna be a winner."

"You've said that after every picture you've taken over the past two hours." Alex laughed. "That thing oughta be running out of film soon."

Tammy shrugged and pushed to her feet. "Maybe. But my boys love cake and I just captured the moment in all its glory. So this one will most definitely be the winner. I already gave Jen your address so she can mail them to us once they're developed."

She returned the camera to the table, then looked around, cheeks heating. Good grief, she hadn't meant to say that. Not yet. And especially not in the flippant way it'd come out, as though she knew he'd be okay with her staying with him longer. But she guessed tonight was as good a time as ever to follow through and tell him how she felt. As a matter of fact, she didn't think a more romantic opportunity could've possibly come along.

Jen and Colt's wedding had been perfect, and the reception was turning out to be just as impressive. Wooden tables, each draped with burlap and lace and decorated with full lilacs in mason jars, surrounded a wide dance floor beneath a clear tent. Softly lit chandeliers and strings of lights hung from the ceiling, and the setting sun cast a rosy glow over the interior, the colorful hues mingling with the starlight emerging overhead.

The hum of cheerful voices, laughter and clicks of cameras filled the elegant space. Tammy smiled. Jen had asked everyone to leave their phones and tablets behind and give their attention to one another instead. The only pictures taken were those by the photographer during the wedding and the ones guests snapped during the reception with the cameras Jen and Colt had provided at each table. As a result, everyone was focused on the happy couple seated at the head table and the ones they loved at their side.

Tammy closed her eyes and sighed. She was lucky enough to have the two people she loved most with her tonight. And it was high time to tell Alex how much she loved him. Tonight was an ideal opportunity.

"Perfect," Tammy whispered.

"That's true from where I'm sitting."

Tammy glanced over her shoulder at the deep rumble and found Alex's eyes roving down her back. An appreciative grin curved his lips and lit his eyes.

Lord, he was handsome. He'd discarded his jacket

and tie long ago, and the top buttons of his blue collared shirt were undone, revealing a tantalizing glimpse of his muscular chest. His salt-and-pepper hair was mussed from Brody playing with it during the wedding, and the dark stubble covering his jaw had deepened throughout the afternoon, giving him an earthy and attractive air.

Tammy turned, pinched the corner of her teal skirt and cocked an eyebrow. "I take it you like my dress?"

His eyes traveled up over her chest to her mouth, then darkened. "I like everything."

His husky voice danced over every inch of her. She breathed in deep and held the warm summer air in her lungs for a moment before gesturing toward his lap. "Is there room for one more?"

His eyes sparkled and he moved to speak, but Brody beat him to it. The baby squealed and beckoned her with his messy fingers.

Alex laughed. "There's your answer."

Smiling, Tammy picked Brody up, sat on Alex's muscular thigh, then cuddled Brody to her chest. As she kissed his cheeks, the baby giggled, then poked his fingers against her mouth, thick crumbs of cake falling from his hands and into the V of her dress.

"No, thank you, Brody," she said. "I've had enough cake." She studied the white icing and red punch stains on Brody's baby tie and slacks. "And I think you have, too." She looked at Alex and laughed. "It's gonna take a fire hose to wash him down tonight. I hope Jen's mom knows what she's getting into."

"Oh, she'll take care of it." Alex pulled them both closer, then ran a broad palm over Brody's shiny hair. "He'll be squeaky clean by the time we get him back in the morning."

His arms tightened around them, and his eyes dimmed.

Tammy studied his face, limbs trembling. She knew what he was thinking. The same thing she was. Brody would have a great time playing with the other children at a sleepover tonight, and it was guaranteed that he'd be back in their arms tomorrow. But what about the days that followed? How much longer would he remain theirs? She'd grown to love him and couldn't imagine life without him.

Her stomach lurched, and she forced her fears down, wanting so much to see Alex smile again.

"We might need to hose you down, as well," Tammy said, eyeing Alex's mouth and leaning closer. "You've got a bit of icing…right here."

His lips were soft and warm beneath hers, the icing melting on her tongue and mingling with his familiar taste as she kissed him. It was as wonderful as she imagined. He groaned, the sexy sound vibrating against her breasts and sending a delicious thrill through her.

"All right. I think it's 'bout time I took that beautiful baby."

Tammy reluctantly pulled away to find Nora Taylor, Jen's mom, lifting Brody from her lap.

"Looks like y'all need a little alone time," Nora said. "We've got a movie, toys and junk food ready inside for the kids, and I'll take great care of this little one."

She began soothing Brody as he whined and twisted, reaching for Tammy.

"Oh, it's okay, sweet boy," Tammy said, standing and kissing Brody. "We're right here and you'll see us in the morning."

Brody quieted down after Alex hugged and kissed him, then smiled again as Meg bounded over. She took his hand and cooed at him as they left the tent, and Brody was laughing before they made it outside.

Tammy forced her feet to stay still, but her heart screamed for her to follow and take Brody back. Her arms felt empty without him. As though a part of her was missing.

"He'll be okay." Alex's whisper tickled her ear and ruffled her hair. He took her hand in his, the gentle strength of his grip releasing some of the tension in her legs and easing her fears. "There's a space on that dance floor just waiting for someone to fill it. Care to dance with me?"

Tammy faced him, noting the sad look in his eyes and tender expression. She didn't know if the offer was an attempt to distract her from the loss of Brody or if he wanted to hold her as much as she longed to hold him. Either way, she'd take it.

"I'd love to."

He smiled, then led the way to the dance floor, taking her in his arms and swaying to the slow beat. She moved closer in his arms, her skirt rustling against his dress slacks.

Each of his movements surrounded her with a heady mixture of his cologne and masculine scent. Excited shivers chased through her. She closed her eyes, pressed her cheek to his chest and savored the strong throb of his heart through the soft cotton of his shirt. His hands drifted lower on her back, then stopped as they reached the curve of her bottom.

He chuckled, his chest vibrating beneath her cheek. "It's a shame we always have an audience."

She raised her head, her breath catching at the dark heat in his eyes. He smiled, then tipped his chin toward the other side of the room. She swiveled in his arms and sifted visually through the couples swaying in time to the music.

Jen and Colt watched them from the head table. They leaned against each other with their arms entwined. Jen had a dreamy expression on her face. Colt smiled, lifted his glass with his free hand and tipped it toward them.

Tammy's chest fluttered. Colt and Jen looked perfect together. Just as perfect as this moment with Alex felt.

She spun back to Alex, slid her arms around his waist and hugged him closer. "If you don't want an audience, why don't you take me to your room?" She met his eyes, smiled up at him, then whispered, "And make love to me? Because I can't think of a better way to end the day."

His chest rose on a swift breath, and his hands cradled her face. "Neither can I."

They left, easing their way through the maze of dancing couples, then crossed the dimly lit fields to the main house. The sun had set and the stars were out, lighting their way. Tammy held Alex's hand tighter as they climbed the front porch steps, then walked down the hall to his room.

Once inside, he toed the door shut behind them, crossed the room and turned on the lamp. He stood still beside it, his eyes heating as they traveled down the length of her. The soft light highlighted the strong curve of his jaw and the sculpted outline of his muscles beneath the fitted dress shirt.

Her belly quivered, nervous tension assaulting her, and the floor dipped beneath her feet. She reached out and placed a palm flat against the wall.

"Tammy."

Her eyes lifted to his, and she melted at the patient concern in his expression, a sudden lightness flooding her.

"This is your call." He shook his head. "We don't have to—"

"No." She smiled, then lifted each foot in turn, removing the dressy boots Jen had loaned her. "I mean yes. I want to."

He smiled, his voice soft as he slid off his tie and tossed it aside. "Then I'm yours. However you want me."

She walked over and unbuttoned his shirt, her fingers trembling as they brushed against his warm skin. Parting the material, she slid it over his broad shoulders and down his arms, letting it fall to the floor. She placed her hands on his wide chest, the sprinkling of hair tickling her palms, then ran them gently over his biceps, his back and, eventually, his muscled abs. They rippled beneath her touch.

A soft groan escaped him, and his eyes closed, his throat moving on a hard swallow.

He was beautiful. More beautiful than any man she'd ever seen. She bit her lip, a wave of heat moving through her as she took his hands in hers. They were so big her palms disappeared beneath his, but there was a gentle stillness in them. One that was protective and kind. As though they were at her bidding.

Her throat tightened, and her heart swelled in her chest, warming her eyes and blurring her vision. She rose to her tiptoes and touched her lips to his, her kiss gentle as she breathed him in and relished the pleasure on his face.

He deepened the contact, his tongue parting her lips

and sweeping against hers. She closed her eyes and gave herself over to his kiss, vaguely registering him removing the rest of their clothing, then walking her backward. The soft corner of the mattress bumped the back of her legs as he guided her gently to the bed.

The warmth of his mouth touched her ankle, then trailed farther up the inside of her leg. His tongue flicked softly against her skin, sending shivers through her. She giggled, then looked down when he teased the back of her knee, her breath snagging at the sight of his dark head between her thighs.

He glanced up, and a slow grin spread across his face as he eased up her body and kissed her. He worked his way back down to her breasts, his attention lingering there. Each strong pull of his mouth overwhelmed her with new, exciting sensations and caused her grip on his shoulders to tighten. When he traveled lower, drifting his mouth across her belly, then lower still, her head dropped back and all thoughts left her.

He rolled away briefly, palmed his wallet from his discarded pants, then returned. He knelt between her thighs, then hesitated, frowning at the protection in his hand.

"Tammy, I…" A flush spread over his face and neck, and his hand shook slightly.

"Wait." Heart slamming against her ribs, she lifted up on her elbow and covered his hand with hers, the foil package cool against her palm. "I guess I need to tell you before we go any further that I've—" Her throat closed, and she swallowed hard, wishing she knew what he was thinking. Wishing his body was still covering hers. "I've never done this before." She laughed, her cheeks burning. "If for no other reason than so you'll be aware. But I don't want you to stop. You make me feel so much. So many things I never knew I could feel."

His eyes shadowed, and he began to pull away.

"Please, Alex," she whispered, hooking an arm around his neck and tugging him back over her. "Please don't think. Just feel."

She kissed him, pouring her soul into it, hoping he could feel what she felt. Could understand how much she loved him.

He closed his eyes and touched his forehead to hers. A muscle ticked in his jaw. "I don't want to hurt you."

She cupped his face and brushed her thumbs over his mouth, loving him more than she'd ever thought possible. "You won't," she whispered.

And he didn't. There was no pain. If anything, she felt safer and more loved than she ever had in her life. He joined his body to hers and moved tenderly, filling her completely, body and soul. The emotions he stirred within her grew so strong they broke free, overtaking them both and spilling down her cheeks.

Afterward, he stilled above her, his heavy breaths dancing over her breasts and ruffling her hair as he stared down at her. His cheeks glistened in the low lamplight, and the same wonder and surprise overwhelming her was reflected in his eyes.

Tammy drew in a shaky breath and wrapped her arms tighter around his muscular back, wanting to hold on to the moment. Wanting to hold on to what she'd never had before.

This is how love should feel.

She smiled, her heart tripping when he returned it. His face creased with pleasure, and they laughed softly. She drifted her fingertips through the tears of joy on his face, losing herself in his warm eyes and glimpsing the beautiful possibilities that awaited them. A home filled with love and laughter. And children. Lots of children. Babies with his beautiful smile who would feel as safe and loved in his arms as she did.

It was the perfect moment to tell him. Absolutely perfect.

"I LOVE YOU."

Alex tried to still the tremors rippling through his limbs at Tammy's words. His body was sated, his mind clear, and his heart strained to hold itself together, the longing welling within it threatening to make it burst.

She'd given him such a gift. One he'd never be able to return. And the sweet words she'd just spoken stoked the fire in his belly, sending a fresh wave of desire through him and urging him to take her again.

She was so beautiful lying there beneath him, cheeks flushed, hair tousled and eyes soft.

He moved to speak, but his throat closed with emotion. His biceps shook on either side of her and his hands curled tighter into the sheets.

"You don't have to say it." Tammy reached up, her fingers fumbling over his lips as her smile widened. "I know. I just want to tell you that I'm willing to make an honest man of you."

He laughed and shook his head, his arms almost giving way beneath him. He rolled to his back before his strength completely left him and tugged her with him, holding her close.

She propped her chin on his chest, her soft breasts pressing against his abs, and drifted her fingers through his hair. "I want to share my life with you."

God, how he wanted that. He wrapped his arms around her and lifted her farther up his body. Her hair spilled over her shoulders and cascaded around his face as he kissed her, her sweet scent filling his senses and the taste of her kiss lingering on his tongue.

"I want to help you rebuild your business." Her green eyes traveled over his face as she smoothed her fingers over his jaw. "I want to rock beside you in those beautiful chairs every day. I want to grow old with you. I want to hold you and kiss you every night."

He grinned and kissed her again, pulling back when she moaned softly. Lord, she was gorgeous. He had no doubts she'd grow only more beautiful over the years. But he, on the other hand…

Alex chuckled. "I'm ten years older than you. Years down the road, after I lose my touch, will you still hold and kiss me? Dentures and all?"

She laughed. "Especially then. Because I have a feeling I'll love you even more, if that's possible." Her eyes softened on his face. "I love you, and I want to make you happy."

He glided his hands in circles across her smooth back. His palms rasped against her soft skin, and his chest swelled with hope at the future she described. He needed so much to hear her say it. To hear her tell him a life together was all she wanted. That it'd be enough.

"This goes both ways," he said, staring into her eyes. "What would make you happy?"

"Hmm." She smiled. "A home with you."

His chest expanded, filling with relief, and he squeezed her tighter.

"And babies," she whispered.

He froze.

"Lots of beautiful babies," she continued, "with your dimples, strength and stubbornness." She laughed. "I want a houseful of rowdy boys that look like you and a couple of feisty girls that look like me."

He held her gaze and fought to keep his smile in place, his chest aching.

She frowned as she studied his expression, her words becoming hesitant. "Do you want that?" Her lips trembled. "Do you want me?"

His throat tightened, and his lungs burned. He hugged her close, eased her cheek to his chest and tucked her head under his chin. "Yes." He struggled to breathe. "I want you."

He winced, the pain streaking through him almost unbearable. He wanted her. More than he'd ever wanted anyone or anything in his life. Loved her more than he'd ever loved anyone before.

But she'd given him so much more than he'd ever be able to give her in return. How the hell could he take even more? Especially when he couldn't give her what *she* wanted?

His gut burned. He ached to tell her, but his throat locked and the words died on his tongue, the thought of her looking at him differently too much to bear. What could he possibly offer her other than an empty house and a future filled with regret?

"I love Brody, too."

He stilled as her soft whisper swept over him.

"I wish he was ours," she added, her warm lips moving against his skin.

Alex clenched his teeth. Brody *was* theirs. They loved Brody as much as he imagined any biological parents could love a son. And the three of them had become a family. *His* family.

Alex closed his eyes and kissed the top of her head, her hair soft against his cheek. He'd drive to Deer Creek first thing when they returned to the ranch Monday. He'd see Maxine, convince her that Brody belonged with him and ask her what he had to do to make it happen.

He couldn't give Tammy a child of her own. But he'd do everything in his power to give her Brody. And he hoped like hell he and Brody would be enough.

Chapter Ten

"Go ahead, Brody." Alex smiled. "Throw 'em a big handful."

Brody looked down at the oats and seeds filling his tiny palm, glanced up at Alex, then pointed with his free hand at the large pond on Raintree Ranch's front lot. "Dat."

"Ducks," Alex said, gesturing toward the dozens of multicolored birds dunking their heads underwater and ruffling their thick feathers. "Those are ducks and they're hungry. Go give 'em some breakfast."

Brody blinked up at him, forehead creasing, then stepped slowly to the edge of the pond. Alex followed, squatted on the thick green grass at Brody's side, then guided his hand forward, sprinkling the food into the water with a soft splash.

He brushed the baby's brown bangs out of his wide eyes as he stared at the ducks. "If you stay really quiet," he whispered, "they'll come grab it."

As if on cue, three ducks on the fringe of the group craned their long necks in their direction, then swam over. They skirted around the floating seeds, then dipped their heads and started eating.

Brody gasped. His brows lifted, and his mouth curved

into an O of surprise. He grabbed Alex's forearm and whispered, "Dat."

"Ducks."

Brody turned Alex's hands over and scowled at his empty palms.

Alex chuckled. "I don't have any more." He turned and pointed behind him. "But Tammy does."

Brody's eyes followed the direction of his hand to where Tammy sat on the grass. He took off, running toward Tammy as fast as his short, chubby legs would carry him.

Tammy held up a plastic bag filled with seeds and waved, urging Brody on. When he reached her, she tipped the bag and poured more seeds into Brody's hand.

Alex admired the gentle way her hand cupped Brody's and the soft smile she gave as she spoke. It was so similar to the one she'd had this morning when he'd drifted kisses over her cheeks and forehead as she slept beside him. Full of love and adoration.

Her eyelids had fluttered open beneath his lips, and she'd tugged his head down to kiss him back. Her soft curves and warm kiss woke him up better than a strong cup of coffee ever could. But he'd had a hard time leaving that bed this morning. So had she. One night with her in his arms wasn't nearly enough, but they'd both been anxious to see Brody and spend their last day at Raintree Ranch together. They'd started touring the ranch right after a big Sunday breakfast, showing Brody the animals and enjoying his reactions to them.

"Get ready," Tammy said, helping Brody turn without spilling his handful of seeds. "He's restocked."

She laughed as Brody toddled over, and a rush of pleasure swept through him at the sound.

"Dat," Brody shouted, stopping at Alex's side.

More ducks had glided over—at least a dozen swam around the edge, pecking the water for more food.

Alex smiled and put a finger to his lips. "You've got to be as quiet as you can—"

"Dat!" Brody slung his hand forward, scattering seeds over the ducks, and squealed.

The ducks scattered, darting wildly in different directions. Brody stopped yelling, pointed at the fleeing animals, then frowned up at Alex. A wounded question formed in his big brown eyes. "Uh-oh."

"That's what happens when you're not quiet around them." Alex picked Brody up and tickled his ribs. "We've got to work on your finesse, son."

Brody giggled and squirmed, then threw his arms around Alex's neck and hugged him.

Son. Alex closed his eyes and rubbed Brody's back. In his heart, that was exactly what Brody had become.

"I wish I still had that camera from last night."

Alex glanced over to find Tammy smiling at them, her knees to her chest and her chin resting on them. Her cheeks were flushed from the heat of the morning sun, and freckles were scattered along the bridge of her nose.

"Nah." He laughed. "You've taken more than enough pictures this weekend."

He crossed to her side and bent, pressing kisses across her cheeks, then down her neck as she tipped her head back with a soft sound of pleasure.

A buzz in his back pocket intruded, and he pulled away with a groan, lowering Brody into her arms. "Hold him for a sec, please? Earl promised he'd call with an update on the horses."

Alex tugged his phone out and took the call, grinning as Brody smooshed Tammy's cheeks and ran his tiny hands through her hair. "Hello."

"Alex. It's Maxine."

His grip tightened on the phone. Several possibilities as to why Maxine had called formed in his mind. But one stood out more than the others.

The sounds of Tammy's and Brody's laughter grew louder, and he turned, focusing on the pond water as it rippled in the warm breeze.

"Are you there, Alex?"

"Yeah. I'm here."

"I hate to call so early in the morning," she said. "Especially when you're out of town. But it was necessary, and I think you know why I'm calling."

His gut roiled.

"John got in touch with me last night." She sighed, the soft sound whispering across the line. "He and his fiancée have decided to take Brody."

Alex clenched his teeth, a pain shooting through his jaw. Last night while he'd made love to Tammy and imagined himself part of a family, his dream was being dismantled by Dean's sorry-ass brother in Boston. A man who hadn't given two thoughts to Dean when he was alive and thought he had a claim to Brody now.

Hell, no.

"He can't have him." Alex winced at the sharp sound of his voice. He regrouped, striving for a calmer tone. "Maxine, I understand John is blood, but I knew Dean. And I know Brody. He's been happy with me and

Tammy." He balled his fist at his side. "Brody belongs with me. It's what Dean would've wanted."

"I know that's what Dean would've wanted had he known what was going to happen." Her voice softened. "But he didn't know, Alex. He didn't plan for anything like this. And John is Brody's family."

"The hell he is." Alex shook his head, his chest burning. "I'm the closest thing Brody has to a family. He's *my* family—" His voice cracked, and he sucked in a ragged breath. "Maxine, please. If there's anything you can do…"

"I'm so sorry." Her words shook. "We both knew this was temporary. I was hoping things would turn out differently, but they didn't. We have no choice. You have to bring Brody back now. John is coming to your place this afternoon to pick him up."

The peaceful scene before Alex blurred, the green field bleeding into the pond. A hollow chasm unfolded inside him, and every dream he ever had fell right through it.

"Think of Brody, Alex." Maxine's tone turned firm. "I know it hurts to lose him, but he'll be going to a good home. And whatever John and Dean's relationship may or may not have been, by all accounts, John is a good man who is doing what he feels is the right thing. He's promised to take good care of Brody. You, of all people, know how precious finding a permanent placement is, and I know you love Brody. So please try to make this transition as easy as possible for him."

Everything turned numb. His chest, his body, his skin. But he managed to speak. "We'll leave right away."

He cut the call, shoved the phone in his pocket, then

flexed his hands, trying to dislodge the stiffness and collect his composure.

"They're taking Brody, aren't they?"

Alex turned, the weak thread in Tammy's voice bringing his eyes to hers. The shadows in her expression and the blissful, unaware grin on Brody's face as he bounced in her lap shot a stabbing pain through him. And he wondered how in the hell he could feel nothing—*and everything*—at the same time.

"Yes."

The drive back was silent, except for Brody's sporadic chatter and giggles from the back of the cab. Alex drove as slowly as possible on the highway, ignoring the cars speeding by and trying to hold on to every last second he had left with Brody. He glanced in the rearview mirror every few minutes, catching a quick glimpse of Brody's shoe kicking the back seat or his tiny fingers lifting as he played. And he tried to make it last forever.

But the miles continued to pass, and when they arrived at the ranch, the late-afternoon sun glinted off an unfamiliar sedan parked in front of the house.

"Is that them already?" Tammy straightened. Her hands gripped the edge of her seat, and her voice hardened. "They'll just have to wait. We haven't packed his things or had a chance to…"

She turned away and looked out the passenger window, her shoulders shaking.

Alex reached out and covered her hand with his, forcing himself to say the words that needed to be said. "He's going to be okay, Tammy."

She faced him. Tears welled over her thick lashes and spilled down her cheeks. "Without us?"

He nodded, his stiff neck protesting the movement. "Without us."

After parking the truck, Alex waited as Tammy removed Brody from his car seat and cradled him to her chest. They walked to the front porch to find Earl standing on the top step with Scout stretched out at his feet. A man and a woman each sat in a rocking chair, visibly anxious.

"Ah, here they are now." Earl nodded at Alex, his smile not reaching his eyes as he whispered, "Hope you don't mind. Maxine called, said they were leaving her office to come out here and asked if I'd hold down the fort with them until you got back."

"Thanks." Alex stepped past him as the couple stood. "John?"

The man moved forward, brushed a blond curl from his forehead and held out his hand. Alex shook it and forced a polite smile. He looked so young. And nothing like Dean.

"It's nice to meet you, Alex." John gestured to the woman who now stood beside him. "This is Becky, my fiancée."

Alex greeted her, then made the rest of the introductions, his throat thickening more with each word. Brody grew frustrated and wiggled in Tammy's arms, straining to get down.

"We've had a long trip," Tammy said, setting Brody on his feet. "He hasn't had a chance to stretch his legs."

Brody scrambled off, climbed into the small rocking chair and leaned forward, smiling as it rocked back, then picked up a steady rhythm. Scout darted over, leaped into his lap and propped his chin on Brody's knees.

Alex flinched, his skin growing clammy. "I need to

pack some of Brody's clothes. And there's a few toys he got for his birthday that he'll want to take with him." He turned and walked toward the door, needing privacy. Needing to be alone. "Tammy will fill you in on what he likes and doesn't like."

Alex made his way to the nursery, praying his legs didn't give out beneath him. It took half an hour to pack a few bags for Brody. Alex's hands shook as he folded small shirts and pants, then packed diapers and toys. When he finished, he stopped on the threshold and took one last look around.

Years ago, he'd stood here after receiving the news of his infertility. Right in this same damned spot, feeling like a failure and less of a man than he ever had. But back then, he didn't have a face to the loss. The children he and Susan had planned to have were just bits of imagination. Hazy thoughts, at best.

But *this*. Losing Brody...

Alex choked back a sob. Then he stepped into the hallway and slammed the door shut. And the hell if he'd ever step foot in that room again.

A few minutes later, Earl said a gruff goodbye to Brody, then left, ambling toward his house. Alex waited by the car with John and Becky, his chest aching as Tammy knelt in front of Brody's rocking chair, speaking softly to him. Brody smiled up at her as she picked him up, then walked over.

"He likes to play in water," Tammy whispered. She kissed Brody's cheek as he nuzzled his face against her chest. "Do you have a swimming pool?"

"No." Becky smiled. "But my mother does. She lives down the road from us."

"That's good." Tammy rubbed a hand over Brody's

back. "He likes long baths, too. And dogs. He loves dogs."

"We'll take good care of him," John said, opening the back door and holding his arms out. "It's time for us to get going. We have a flight to catch."

Tammy nodded. She bit her lip and leaned over to pass Brody to John. "This is John, Brody. He and Ms. Becky are going to take good care of you."

Brody lifted his head, looked up at John, then back at Tammy. His brow creased with confusion. John reached out, and Brody shrank back, hiding his face in Tammy's throat and issuing short cries of panic.

Alex gritted his teeth. His hands clenched at his sides as Tammy tugged at Brody's arms and tried to coax him into going to John. Brody refused, his wails growing shriller.

"It's okay, Brody," Tammy said, wincing as Brody's fingers tangled in her hair and pulled. Her eyes welled with tears, and she glanced at Alex helplessly, her voice breaking. "He won't let go."

Grimacing, Alex moved close and took Brody's hands in his. He gently unwound Brody's fingers from Tammy's hair, then forcibly removed him from her arms. Brody stiffened and cried out, the sound piercing Alex's ears and cracking his heart.

"It's okay," Alex whispered against Brody's ear as he passed him to John. He inhaled Brody's soft baby scent, holding it in his lungs and imprinting it on his heart. "You're gonna be okay, Brody."

John and Becky scrambled to get Brody settled in his car seat and shut the door. Brody sobbed louder, the sound echoing within the car.

"Thanks for taking care of him," John said hastily, climbing in the driver's seat.

Becky gave a pained smile, then slid in the passenger seat. The engine turned over, and they pulled away, dust billowing up behind the car as they disappeared down the driveway. Scout followed for several feet, barking, then eventually turned and darted into a field to snuffle around in the grass.

It was quiet for a few moments. Then Tammy's sobs broke the silence, filling the emptiness surrounding them.

Alex pulled her to him, wrapping his arms around her and holding her tight. Her fists dug into his back and her hot tears scalded his throat, each of her cries cutting deeper into his chest.

And he knew, without a doubt, that he could no longer offer her the family she dreamed of and deserved. That he could never truly make her happy.

He closed his eyes as her sobs grew louder. God, he couldn't go through this again. He couldn't let Tammy stay with him out of a sense of duty like Susan had, only to see her smile fade and regret haunt her eyes. He wouldn't be able to survive it. He loved her too much.

Enough to do the right thing? To make her happy? Whatever it takes?

He cringed. At least he could do the right thing this time, the only thing he could do to ensure she had a shot at getting the future—and happiness—she deserved. And the longer he put it off, the harder it would be.

Alex waited until she grew quiet again, the shudders sweeping through her body easing and her hold on him loosening. He eased back and lifted her chin with his knuckle, swallowing hard at the trails of tears on her cheeks and feeling completely dead inside.

"This is the end of our deal, Tammy."

TAMMY BLINKED, HER EYES hot and gritty, and tried to fight her way out from under the pain of losing Brody. Tried to focus on Alex.

He stared down at her, his expression grim and his eyes empty.

"What did you just say?"

His hands moved, cupping her jaw, and his thumbs brushed over her cheeks. "I said this is the end of our deal." His chest lifted on a sharp inhale. "It's time for you and Razz to leave."

A laugh burst from her lips. She cringed at the bitterness of it and grabbed Alex's wrists, tugging them away from her face. "I'm going to forgive you for this later," she said, blinking back a fresh surge of tears. "Because I know you're hurting right now. And I know that's where this is coming from." She shook her head. "But for now, we're going to go inside, crawl in bed together and cry. And when we can't cry anymore, we're going to get up, take a shower and wash this day away. Then we'll start over. Together."

He pulled away and rubbed his hands over his jeans. "I don't have another fresh start in me."

Tammy balled her fists, her legs weakening. "Look, these past few hours have been a nightmare for both of us. But this pain won't last forever. It'll pass. It'll blow over and we'll survive it."

"No, we won't." He dragged a hand over his face and looked away, his wide shoulders sagging. "I can't give you what you want."

"You're not making sense, Alex." She scrubbed the back of her hand over her cheeks. "I told you what I wanted last night. I want you. I want—"

"A home with me?" He faced her, his gray eyes piercing. "And children?"

"Yes." Her throat ached, and a heavy weight pressed on her chest. "We may have lost Brody, but there'll be other children once we recover from this." She pressed her palms to his chest, searching for the strong throb of his heart. "We'll make them together. As many as we want."

His muscles tensed beneath her touch, his expression darkening. "I can't give you children."

Tammy froze. "What?"

Alex covered her hands with his and searched her face. "That's why Susan left. It's what I couldn't give her." His eyes narrowed as he stared down at her. "If you stay with me, that nursery will remain empty. You'll never be able to get pregnant. You'll never be able to give birth to your own baby, and you'll never see yourself reflected in a child." His boot scraped across the ground as he shifted, squeezing her hands hard. "Can you honestly tell me that's what you want? That just having me would be enough?"

The ground warped beneath her, and her head spun, the pain streaking inside her becoming more intense. She closed her eyes and pulled her hands away, pressing them tight to her middle.

Her mind raced, and she scrambled to focus. To comprehend what he was saying.

They'd never be able to have children. Would never have babies with Alex's smile or her eyes. Would never be able to watch them grow and know they'd left a small part of themselves behind in the world.

She'd never have the family she'd longed for as a girl. And Alex would never hold a son of his own.

Her stomach heaved. It was almost too much to conceive.

"There's nothing for you here, Tammy." His tone turned hard as she opened her eyes. "Nothing but an empty house and beat-up land. You saw it the day we met." His lips twisted, warped and empty. "I'm broken."

Your smile. I thought it looked broken...

Tammy's hands flew to her face and covered her mouth, her teeth biting her lip. "Oh, God. I wish I'd never said that to you." The sharp tang of blood touched her tongue, and she swallowed hard, her cheeks flaming. "I didn't mean it." She shook her head and her hair fell into her eyes, obscuring him. She pushed it back and reached for him. "It's not true."

He stepped back, shoving his hands in his pockets and jerking away.

"This thing between us..." He frowned. "It's a result of circumstance. If we hadn't gone through what we did—" He winced. "If I hadn't helped you like I did and if we hadn't found Brody, you'd have left long ago. You'd have seen me the same way you saw every other man."

"That's not true," she repeated. "I love you and you love me. I know you do." She widened her stance and dug deep, keeping her words solid and firm. "We both have ugly pasts, Alex, and we may not have the future we wanted. But we can build one that'll be ours. What we make of it. And it can be beautiful—"

"Nothing can be built here," he bit out. His eyes

drifted toward the road. Toward the wreckage of Dean and Gloria's house. "This place doesn't breathe. Everything just dies."

"Brody and Razz didn't." Tears streamed down her face. "And neither did we."

His attention returned to her, and his expression softened, the pain etched into his features making her heart bleed.

"My chance for happiness has passed," he whispered. "My dreams died years ago. But you're so young, you still have a shot at yours. I won't take away your chance to be happy. I won't give you a future filled with regret." He flinched. "You'll fall in love again and you'll have children. You'll build the home and family you've always wanted. And you'll be happy."

"Not without you." She held her breath, fighting off a sob. "I don't want any of that if it means losing you. I know you want me, Alex. I know you love me."

"Then let me do the right thing." He walked over, cradled her face with his hands and touched his lips to her forehead. "Let me let you go."

"Alex—"

He dipped his head and took her mouth, his kiss deep and gentle. She wrapped her arms around him and held as tight as she could, but he slipped away, moving toward the house.

Soon, he'd be gone. Just like Brody.

"You're not doing this for me, Alex," she called out as he walked away. "You're doing this for yourself because you're afraid. You've been so worried about my fears, but you're the one who's afraid. You're afraid to take a chance and trust me. Afraid to believe that you're enough. But there's no way I can prove that to you. You have to believe it yourself before you can ever accept it from me."

He didn't respond. Or look back.

"Alex." She shook where she stood, struggling to stay upright as he made his way up the front porch steps. "You said you'd never hurt me."

He jerked to a halt, his broad back stiffening.

"This hurts." Her throat closed, and she forced herself to speak, hoping he'd cave. "It hurts so much. More than anything else ever has."

His head dropped forward as he half turned. The line of his muscular profile sagged, growing weak and defeated as he repeated her own words, his voice strained. "It'll pass."

He entered the house, closing the door behind him and effectively shutting her out.

Tammy stood still until the sun began to set, the darkness creeping over the silent fields and enveloping her. And there was nothing left to do but leave.

She went inside and packed her bags, then she hooked up her trailer and loaded Razz. She climbed into the driver's seat, revved the engine, then drove down the winding driveway until she reached the paved road.

The headlights flooded the land in front of her as she stopped the truck, casting shadows over Dean and Gloria's crumbled home. She looked to either side of her, but the fading fringes of light didn't reach very far, leaving the road dark and indistinguishable in each direction.

Her hands tightened around the steering wheel, and she closed her eyes, knowing the circuit was waiting for her on one end of the highway and Colt and Jen at the other. But neither destination seemed right. And neither path felt the same as it had before.

She didn't feel the same. Her heart, broken into jagged pieces, stabbed sharply within her chest. Her arms felt awkward and empty without Brody. Even her body felt different, Alex's tender touches and movements from last night still lingering deep inside her.

Tammy opened her eyes, hot tears scalding her cheeks, and realized Alex was right about one thing. Like every painful event in her life, this one would pass, too. Only this time, she didn't want to move on. And she had no idea which way to go.

Chapter Eleven

"Finishing up early tonight?"

Tammy scraped the shovel across the stall floor, shook out the clean shavings, then dumped the last bit of manure in the wheelbarrow beside her. Sweat trickled down her cheeks and back. She dragged her arm across her forehead, glanced at the man standing in the entry of the stall and smiled.

"Yeah." She propped the shovel against her hip and tugged her gloves off. "This is the last one. I've already done the rest."

She shoved the worn gloves in her back pocket, rolled her head from side to side to stretch her aching neck and laughed. The *rest* included the other fourteen stalls that were on her job detail as a hand for Red Fox Ranch in Jasper, Georgia. Sixty-five acres and a steady stream of horses to board guaranteed her consistent work and pay.

"I've just finished, too." The man grinned and propped his arm on the stall door. "I was thinking about driving into town and getting a beer. Maybe shooting a few rounds of pool. Care to join me?"

Keith Brinson was a ranch hand, same age as Tammy, who'd flirted with her every night since she'd arrived a month ago. He was blond haired, blue eyed and hand-some. And harmless enough.

"I'm standing next to a cart of manure, am sweaty as a pig and probably stink to high heaven." Tammy cocked an eyebrow. "And you're still asking me out?"

"Yep." His blue eyes drifted over her briefly, then returned to her face. "Doesn't matter when I catch you. You're always beautiful."

She dipped her head and smiled. Keith was a good man. One of those rare gentlemen who still knew how to treat a lady. A woman would be lucky to grace his arm.

Her smile slipped, stormy gray eyes and deep dimples intruding into her thoughts. Just as they had every day over the past month since leaving Deer Creek.

Keith wasn't for her. Her heart still belonged to Alex. Always would.

"Thank you, Keith, but—"

"But you'd rather not." He winced good-naturedly. "I kinda figured that, since you've turned me down every time I've asked." He shrugged. "You taking Razz out tonight, as usual?"

She nodded, glancing toward the open stable doors. It was a beautiful late-September night. "It's cool out and she loves an evening stroll."

That had become Tammy's favorite part of the day, too, since she'd retired from racing and settled in at Red Fox Ranch. She no longer felt the need to run or dreaded being alone. Instead, she enjoyed sitting on the tailgate of her truck in an empty field, watching Razz frolic and gazing at the stars. It helped her feel closer to Alex somehow. Made her think there was a chance he was outside, too. Maybe sitting in one of the rocking chairs on his front porch, looking up and thinking of her…and Brody.

An ache formed in her chest. The same one that returned every time she thought of Brody. It was fruitless, really—thinking of him like she did. But she couldn't help but wonder where he was and what he was doing. If he was happy and safe.

Tammy sighed and eased past Keith, saying goodnight as she made her way to Razz's stall. She guessed that was what being a parent was like—worrying about your children when you weren't with them. And that was how she still felt about Brody. He still belonged to her and Alex. No matter where he was or who was taking care of him.

A half hour later, she sat on the tailgate of her truck in Razz's favorite field and tipped her head back, taking in the moonlit sky above her and wondering if Brody still thought of her. If he still thought of Alex and missed them both.

She lifted her hip, pulled her phone from her back pocket, then dialed the same number she'd dialed several times since Alex had sent her away. It didn't ring. Just went straight to Alex's voice mail as usual.

"Hey. It's me again." She licked her lips and shifted on the tailgate. "You know if you get tired of these messages, you ought to answer your phone at least once and tell me to bug off." She laughed, the sound thin and weak even to her own ears. "It'd save us both a lot of…"

Grief. She cringed. That was the word she was going to say, but it didn't fit. Being apart from Alex hurt no matter what the circumstances. And grief didn't quite cover it.

"Anyway, I thought I'd let you know in case you do decide to call that I'm going off the grid for the weekend starting tomorrow." She swung her legs, watching as her boots skimmed the top of the tall grass. "I'm driving to Raintree to visit Jen and Colt for a couple of days, and she wants my full attention. She said she has news she wants to share in person. I'm thinking she's probably going to tell me that she's adding to the family." She stopped swinging her legs and gripped the hard metal edge of the tailgate. "Just in case you're wondering, I'm happy for her. And I don't envy her." She pulled in a strong breath. "But I do still miss you. And I still love you."

She thought of saying goodbye. Thought of telling him this would be the last time she called. But her heart wasn't ready for that yet. So she cut the call and laid the phone beside her, wishing she could let go of Alex as easily as he had let go of her.

"Looks like it's just us again tonight, girl."

Razz tossed her head, her shiny mane rippling under the starlight, and trotted off, taking full advantage of the energetic thrill buzzing through the cool breeze in the air.

Tammy sighed and managed a small smile. Summer was definitely over.

A clatter started at her side, and she glanced down. Her phone vibrated harder, skipping across the tailgate. She snatched it up.

"Alex?"

Silence greeted her, then, "Tammy?"

Her shoulders sagged at the sound of a female voice. "You got her. Who's this?"

"It's Maxine."

Tammy hopped off the tailgate. "Maxine? Is everything okay?"

"Well, I hope so," she said. "I've been trying to reach

Alex for several days now, and I can't seem to get him to answer the phone or return my calls. And he didn't answer the door when I stopped by." She blew out a breath. "I know he's there. Earl told me he walked over several times to lend a hand with the ranch, but he said Alex barely speaks."

Tammy's stomach churned. "But Alex is okay otherwise?"

"Yes, of course," Maxine said. "He's just being more stubborn than usual."

"Tell me about it," Tammy muttered under her breath.

"What was that?"

"Nothing. What can I do for you, Maxine?"

"Are you still in Georgia?"

"Yeah," Tammy said. "Jasper."

"Good." Maxine cleared her throat. "Actually, Brody is the reason I'm calling."

Tammy froze, a chill sweeping over her skin. "Brody? What's happened? Is he okay?"

"He's fine," Maxine said hastily. "There's no need to worry. It's just that John called last week and said he and Becky were having a tough time adjusting." She paused, the silence rankling Tammy's nerves even more. "I think it was just too much too soon for them. They were ready for marriage but not for a family. Not yet. And John felt awful about it. He said they thought about giving it more time but that they just aren't ready to be parents."

Tammy reached out and gripped the edge of the truck bed, her heart thumping painfully in her chest.

"I was hoping to get in touch with Alex, but since I couldn't reach him, I thought I'd give you a call." Maxine breathed deep over the phone. "Brody is staying at the home in Atlanta and needs to be placed with a foster parent. We have several options for him, but I couldn't help but think of you." Maxine hesitated. "I know things didn't work out with you and Alex, but I know you love Brody. And since you took such good care of him before, I thought—"

"How soon can I have him?"

Maxine laughed. "Slow down. Are you still touring or do you have a permanent place to stay?"

"Yes." Tammy shook her hand and tried to collect her scattered thoughts. "I mean, no, I'm not touring. And I do have a permanent place."

She winced, a pang of discomfort dimming her excitement. She'd prefer to return to Alex, but considering the circumstances, Raintree Ranch would do just fine. Colt and Jen had made it clear over the past weeks that she was more than welcome.

"You'll have to start as a foster parent," Maxine said. "Then after some time, you can apply for adoption. I'll draw up the paperwork tonight and pull a few strings first thing in the morning. Can you make it to Atlanta before three tomorrow?"

Tammy smiled, tears welling onto her lashes. "I'm already on the way."

By one o'clock the next afternoon, after a pile of paperwork and a background check, Tammy stood in the waiting room of the Atlanta children's home, wringing her hands and waiting for Brody to arrive.

"What if he doesn't remember me?" Tammy paced and eyed the closed door to the corridor.

"Relax, Tammy," Maxine said from her seated position across the room. "Everything will be fine."

"But it's been a whole month since I last saw him. He probably won't—"

The door creaked open, and Tammy spun around, clamping her mouth shut. A woman walked in with Brody in her arms. His eyes were heavy, and he looked around the room slowly, as though he'd just woken up from a nap.

"Brody?" Tammy held her breath, her lungs burning as his head swiveled in her direction.

Brody blinked, then his eyes widened, recognition dawning on his face. He squealed and reached out to her, wiggling in the woman's grasp. She set him on his feet, and he toddled over as fast as his little legs would go, his smile bright.

Tammy knelt and opened her arms, catching him as he barreled into her middle. She picked him up and hugged him close, closing her eyes as he laid his head on her chest and sighed contentedly. She breathed him in, savoring the feel of him in her arms and the comforting weight of him over her heart.

"I'm here, Brody," she whispered. "I'm here now. For good."

Tammy smiled, her broken heart beginning to heal. Alex might not allow her to love him, but she would still be able to love Brody.

A BODY RESTS easier after doing the right thing.

Head pounding, Alex groaned and covered his eyes with his hand, avoiding the nagging phrase and struggling to slip back into oblivion. "That's a damned lie."

The pounding grew louder and more painful. He flinched and tried to find a more comfortable position, the wood of the table hard and cold against his cheek.

"Alex?"

More pounding.

"I know you're in there, and if you don't open this door in the next three seconds, I'm gonna kick the damned thing down."

Earl. That was Earl yelling—and pounding.

Alex grunted and cracked his eyes open to peer through the part in his fingers. Sunlight poured through the windows and flooded the kitchen, glinting sharply off the empty glass bottles littering the floor.

"One."

Alex laid his hands flat on the table, shoved himself upright and scrambled to his feet.

"Two."

"I'm coming."

His throat was so dry his words cracked. Which was a hell of a thing, since he'd drunk enough whiskey last night to drown a cow.

"Thr—"

"I said I'm coming."

He stumbled his way to the front door, unlocked it, then jerked it open. The sun scorched his eyes, and he shrank back, squinting and trying to bring Earl into focus.

Earl eyed him from head to toe, then frowned. "You look like hell, son."

Alex scoffed. "Thanks."

Undeterred, Earl shoved past him, clutching a small bundle under his arm, and walked into the kitchen. He stopped in the center of the room and glanced around. "And this room looks worse."

Alex dragged a hand over his face and sighed. "Well,

hell, Earl. You think all these compliments can wait until at least after noon?"

"It is after noon," Earl said, kicking a bottle and watching it spin off with a clang. "It's two o'clock, in fact. You've slept half the day away and who knows how many others since you've holed yourself up in here."

Alex rubbed his temples. "I've just needed some time alone."

"I know." Earl nodded. "I've been tending to your horses while you've had plenty of it over the past month. Helped any, has it?"

Alex winced. No. It hadn't. He'd cut his phone off, ignored his messages and avoided visitors, hoping to return to the status quo. But he missed Tammy and Brody more now than he had weeks ago. And the solitude was no longer comforting. It was just damned lonely.

Earl harrumphed. "It's about time you stop wallowing around in this self-pity of yours and do something productive."

"I'm not wallowing," Alex said. "I'm just…"

"Hiding?"

"No." Alex scowled and shoved his fists in his pockets. "I've been trying to do the right thing."

Earl's eyes narrowed. "By tossing Tammy out?"

Alex flinched. "I didn't toss her out. I asked her to leave."

"Why?"

Alex yanked out a chair with his boot, then sat down and rubbed his forehead.

"Not gonna tell me, huh?" Earl shrugged. "Doesn't matter why. Just tell me this—does it feel right?"

Alex's head shot up, a sharp pain shooting through his neck. "What did you say?"

"Does it feel like you're doing the right thing? 'Cause from where I'm standing, it sure as hell doesn't look like it."

"You don't know anything about it," Alex said, ducking his head at the intense gleam in Earl's eyes and focusing on the rumpled edge of his collar instead.

Earl nodded. "Maybe not. But I know you miss Tammy." His eyes softened. "And Brody. I also know what you're doing now isn't doing you a bit of good."

Alex sighed and sagged back in the chair. "Then what would you suggest I do?"

"Well, for starters, you can get your ass up, drink a pot of coffee and check your mail."

Earl grabbed the bundle from under his arm and threw it. It slammed into Alex's chest and bounced into his lap. A large manila envelope slid off the top of the stack. Alex grabbed it before it fell to the floor.

"Then," Earl continued, "you can clean this mess up and come check on your horses." He smiled. "After that, I might consider inviting you over for supper. You're pretty decent company when you're not hungover."

Alex's mouth quirked. He gathered up the stack of mail, dropped it on the table and started sifting through bills.

"That's the spirit. I'm coming back to check on you to be sure you make it to the coffee." Earl chuckled and headed for the door. He paused on the threshold and turned back, hesitating. "You know, I spent a lot of years alone. I was fine on my own and never needed anyone. Only thing is, I never thought about whether or not someone might need me." He sighed. "I know it hit you hard when Susan left, so I can imagine it was scary letting Tammy in like you did. But the way I see it, if you did decide to take a chance with Tammy and things fell apart, well, it couldn't hurt any worse than it does now, could it?"

Alex froze, his stomach sinking at the words.

The door thudded shut on Earl's exit, and Alex blinked, refocusing on the manila envelope in his hand. It was addressed to him and Tammy.

Alex's hands shook as he studied the postmark. It'd arrived three weeks ago from Raintree, Georgia. Mrs. Jen Mead was listed on the return address. He turned it over, opened it and dumped out the contents.

Dozens of pictures slid across the table, scattering in different directions. All of them had been taken at Jen and Colt's wedding, and every single one of them had Brody in it.

He slumped into a chair, thumbing through them. There were so many. A few he remembered taking of Brody with Tammy as the baby smiled up at her or hugged her neck. All the rest were of him and Brody.

Alex smiled, recognizing the camera angle from when Tammy had knelt in front of them to take the picture or stood over them, cajoling bigger smiles. Even the winner—as Tammy had dubbed it—was there. Brody, the spitting image of Dean, sat on Alex's lap, grinning, his hands covered in icing and frozen halfway to his mouth.

Alex's gut churned, and he looked away, his gaze snagging on a small note among the pictures. He plucked it from the pile and read it.

Hi, Alex.
Colt told me I'm overstepping my boundaries by writing to you. And I know Tammy will kill me

if she ever finds out. But heck, I've always gone
for broke and I want Tammy to be happy. So here
it is—you screwed up. Big-time. And if you're
as smart as I think you are, you'll make it up to
Tammy. Sooner rather than later. Because she's
a wonderful woman who deserves the best. And
after seeing the two of you together, I know without a doubt that you *are* the best. She shines when
she's with you. Go see her, talk to her and you'll
understand. (But please don't feel obligated to tell
her that I wrote you. Did I mention she'd kill me
if she ever found out?)

Alex laughed, the paper shaking in his hand.

I've enclosed pictures from the wedding. I
promised to mail them to Tammy, but I'm hoping
you'll pass them along to her instead. I took the
liberty of enlarging one. Colt took it, and it was
my favorite. It's proof you're a handsome man,
Alex. And I've never seen Tammy happier.
Jen

Alex glanced over the pictures covering the table,
then retrieved the manila envelope and felt inside, finding a larger picture. He tugged it out and laid it on the
table.

Brody wasn't in this one.

A wave of heat swept through Alex, blurring his vision. He blinked hard and studied the picture closer.

Tammy stood on the dance floor in her teal dress,
her arms around his waist and her face tipped up toward his. Her eyes were on him, bright and beautiful,

and her smile was gentle. His hands cradled her face as he looked down at her, his smile just as wide as hers and both of their expressions full of love.

Alex stilled, remembering it clearly. It was the moment after Tammy had asked him to take her to his room and make love to her.

...I can't think of a better way to end the day.

He smiled, wet heat streaming down his cheeks as he whispered, "Neither can I."

God, she was beautiful. And *happy*. So damned happy. *Because of him.*

He held his breath and trailed a finger over her smile. She hadn't been happy in that moment because of Brody. Or because of another baby. She'd been happy because she was with him.

And he was a lucky bastard.

Alex exhaled, then let out a burst of laughter.

"Aw, hell. You didn't dive back into the liquor instead of the coffee, did you?"

Alex spun in his seat, steadied himself with the back of the chair, then scrubbed a hand over his face. Earl stood in the doorway, a look of trepidation crossing his face while Scout nipped at his ankle.

Alex shoved to his feet, shook his head and smiled. "I'm a lucky bastard."

He stopped, suddenly afraid. Just as Tammy had said. He'd focused more on what he couldn't give her than what he could. What he *could* do was love her better than any other man walking the earth. Loving her felt right. Instead, he'd sent her away, believing he wasn't enough.

"And I'm a dumb bastard," he spat, scrambling to regroup.

Earl's eyebrows rose, lips twitching. "I won't argue either point with you."

"You mind if I take a rain check on that dinner tonight?" Alex scooped the pictures up, tidied them back into the envelope, then began picking the empty bottles up off the floor. "I need to straighten up, see about the horses, then take off."

"Where you headed?"

Alex paused, clutching the bottles to his chest. "Wherever Tammy is."

Earl smiled. "I'm all for that. But you're not going anywhere until you drink some coffee, shower and shave. Otherwise, she'll unhook you and throw you right back in the pond."

Alex laughed, a weight lifting from him. "I've got to find her first."

Earl gestured toward the cell phone sticking out from underneath a pile of trash on the table. "Why don't you start by giving her a call?"

He did. But she didn't answer. It rang several times, then kicked to voice mail. He couldn't leave a message. What he wanted to say needed to be said in person.

She'd left him messages, though. He played each one several times as he cleaned up, shaved and packed a bag. She'd called so many times, asking him to pick up or call back, and she'd ended each one with the same phrase.

I still love you.

Lord, he hoped so. He hoped she still loved him despite him acting like a crazy, selfish bastard. And if she didn't, he'd do anything he damned well had to do to earn it back.

The last message was from three days ago and she'd

mentioned visiting Jen at Raintree Ranch. It was the best lead he had, so he started there. He asked Earl to tend to his horses for a few more days, threw his bag in his truck, then headed out, taking the straightest shot he could to Raintree.

The sun was just beginning to set when he arrived. He drove past the main guesthouse to Colt and Jen's house on the back lot, hoping Tammy was still there. He turned onto the driveway, and his headlights illuminated Tammy's truck and trailer parked at the end of it.

His heart lurched. He parked the truck, hopped out and strode up to the front door, running his clammy palms down the sides of his pant legs. He hesitated, then raised his fist and knocked, his knees shaking when footsteps approached.

The door swung open, and the welcoming smile on Jen's face melted away, a cool expression taking its place.

"Hi, Jen."

"Alex." She propped a hand on her hip. "What can I do for you?"

"I'm here to see Tammy."

"Oh, really?" Her eyes narrowed, swept down his frame, then back up again, her gaze lingering on the slight tremble of his hands at his sides. "What for?"

Alex winced. "I screwed up. And I want to make it up to her." He swallowed the tight knot in his throat. "Please, Jen."

A slow smile spread across her face. "It's about time." She turned her head to the side and shouted, "Tammy, get your cute butt down here. You have a guest."

Alex smiled, mouthing *thank you*.

"You're gonna pay me back," Jen whispered, pointing

a finger at his chest and grinning. "You better have that matron of honor position on lock for me."

He nodded, and she left. Footfalls sounded down the stairs, then he heard a murmur of voices from inside. He looked down and dragged a boot over the porch floor, trying to calm his nerves. A pair of boots appeared in front of his, smaller and feminine.

Alex looked up, his heart aching at the guarded look on Tammy's face. "Hey."

She crossed her arms over her chest, her full breasts lifting and her tempting mouth firming.

Every muscle in his body strained to reach out and pull her close. He shifted his stance and cleared his throat. "I needed to see you. I needed to tell you I'm sorry."

Her beautiful eyes flashed. "For what?"

"For ending things the way I did and not having more faith in you. For not being even half as brave as you've been." He sucked in a deep breath. "See, the thing is, everyone keeps thinking it's me who rescued you. But you're the one who rescued me. And I want to return the favor."

She stayed silent, her expression softening.

"I want to offer you a deal." He stepped forward and looked down at her, the warmth radiating from her soft curves making him long to lean closer. "I can't give you children. And I can't—"

His voice broke, and he looked away, fighting back the wave of grief washing over him.

"I can't give you Brody," he forced out, flinching. "But I can give you my heart. Every corner of it." He faced her, peering into her eyes. "I can give you a life full of love, laughter and time spent together. I love you. I want to marry you and share my life with you. I want to rock beside you on the front porch every day and hold and kiss you every night. And I swear I'll love you better than any other man ever could. Every day. For the rest of our lives."

Her lower lip trembled. "You want to kiss me every night? For the rest of our lives?"

He nodded, leaning closer. "Yes."

She smiled, small and shaky, and tears escaped her lashes. "Dentures and all?"

He laughed, his own eyes tearing up, and cradled her face in his hands. "Yes."

Tammy's smile faded. She uncrossed her arms, then wrapped her hands around his wrists. "I can only accept on one condition."

Alex straightened, his heart pounding. "Anything."

She sighed. "I come with a lot of baggage, and you have to agree to take it on, too."

"I will." He dipped his head and kissed her, eager for the sweet taste of her again. She melted into him, and at her soft moan, he lifted his head and whispered, "Whatever it is."

She smiled, then slipped out of his arms. He immediately followed, reaching for her as she turned her head and beckoned someone with her hand.

"Come on," she said, laughing.

A familiar cackle rang out. Alex stopped and turned his head to the side.

Brody, clad in baby jeans and a T-shirt, ran toward them, hair flopping and diaper swishing with each step.

Alex sank to his knees and held out his arms. "Brody?"

Brody's brown eyes lit up as he spotted Alex. "Dat!"

He darted over, wrapped his arms around Alex's neck and squealed, his legs lifting restlessly in a demand to be picked up.

"John and Becky changed their minds." Tammy smiled softly as Alex stood with Brody in his arms. "It wasn't the right time for them." She stepped forward and touched his forearm. "But I think it's just the right time for us."

Alex pulled her close and wrapped them both in his arms, laughing and crying at the same time. "It's the perfect time," he whispered. "Just perfect."

Tammy hugged him back, kissed Brody's cheek and asked, "Can we go home now?"

Alex nodded, his heart full to bursting. "Yeah. We're going home."

Brody laid his head on Alex's chest, right over his heart. Alex kissed Tammy again and held his family in a protective embrace, savoring every moment. And he knew he was right where he belonged.

* * * * *

If you loved this book, don't miss April Arrington's other MEN OF RAINTREE RANCH *books:*

TWINS FOR THE BULL RIDER
THE RANCHER'S WIFE
THE BULL RIDER'S COWGIRL

Get 2 Free Books,

By the time her mom rang the bell signaling lunch was ready, Sloane had learned that Jason was from Idaho, he'd been competing as a professional since he was eighteen and he'd had six broken bones thanks to his career choice.

"Are you eating with us?" Phoebe asked as she slipped her little hand into Jason's.

He smiled down at her. "I don't think they planned for the extra mouth to feed."

Sloane huffed at that. "You've never met my mother and her penchant for making twice as much food as needed."

"Please," Phoebe said.

"Well, how can I say no to such a nice invitation?"

Phoebe gave him a huge smile and shot off toward the picnic area.

Jason chuckled. "Sweet kids."

"Yeah. And resilient."

He gave her a questioning look.

"They come from tough backgrounds. All of them have had to face more than they should at their age."

"That's sad."

"It is. They seem to like you, though."

"And that annoys you."

"I didn't say that."

"You didn't have to." He grinned at her as he grabbed a ham-and-cheese sandwich and a couple of her mom's homemade oatmeal cookies.

"Sorry. I just don't know you, and these kids' safety is my responsibility."

"So this has nothing to do with the fact your sister is trying to set us up?"

"Well, there goes my hope that it was obvious only to me."

"It's not a bad idea. I'm a decent guy."

"Perhaps you are, but you're also going to be long gone by tomorrow night."

He nodded. "Fair enough."

Well, that reaction was unexpected. She'd thought he might try to encourage her to live a little, have some harmless fun. She wasn't a fuddy-duddy, but she also wasn't hot on the idea of being with a guy who'd no doubt been with several women before her and would be with several afterward.

Of course, she often doubted a serious relationship was for her either. She'd seen at a young age what loving someone too much could do to a person. The one time she'd believed she might have a future with a guy, she'd been proved wrong in a way that still stung years later.

Don't miss HER TEXAS RODEO COWBOY
by Trish Milburn, available September 2017
wherever Harlequin® Western Romance
books and ebooks are sold.

www.Harlequin.com

EXCLUSIVE LIMITED TIME OFFER AT
www.HARLEQUIN.com

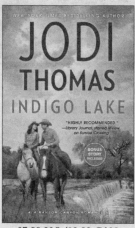

$7.99 U.S./$9.99 CAN.

$1.⁰⁰ OFF

New York Times Bestselling Author
JODI THOMAS

INDIGO LAKE

Two families long divided by an ancient feud. Can a powerful love finally unite them?

Available July 18, 2017.
Get your copy today!

Receive **$1.00 OFF** the purchase price of
INDIGO LAKE by Jodi Thomas
when you use the coupon code below on Harlequin.com.

INDIGO1

Offer valid from July 18, 2017, until August 31, 2017, on www.Harlequin.com.

Valid in the U.S.A. and Canada only. To redeem this offer, please add the print or ebook version of INDIGO LAKE by Jodi Thomas to your shopping cart and then enter the coupon code at checkout.

H
HQN™
www.HQNBooks.com

PHCOUPJT0817

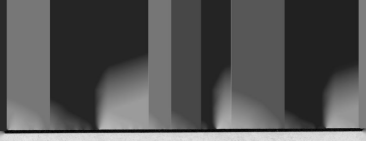

Earn points from all your Harlequin book purchases from wherever you shop.

Turn your points into *FREE BOOKS* of your choice
OR
EXCLUSIVE GIFTS from your favorite authors or series.

Join for FREE today at
www.HarlequinMyRewards.com.

Harlequin My Rewards is a free program (no fees) without any commitments or obligations.

MYR17